TWIN PURSUITS

ESCAPE to Deer Island

JEANETTE WINDLE

ESCAPE TO DEER ISLAND

published by Multnomah Books
a part of the Questar publishing family

© 1996 by JEANETTE WINDLE

International Standard Book Number: 0-88070-906-5

Cover illustration by xxx

Printed in the United States of America.

For information:
QUESTAR PUBLISHERS, INC.
POST OFFICE BOX 1720
SISTERS, OREGON 97759

Library of Congress Cataloging-in-Publication Data:

Windle, Jeanette.
   Escape to Deer Island / by Jeanette Windle.
      p. cm. — (Twin pursuits)
   Summary: After a mysterious man suggests that their father may be selling infor-
mation to a Middle Eastern terrorist, the twins become entangled in international
espionage.
   ISBN 0-88070-906-5 (alk. paper)
   [1. Robbers and outlaws—Fiction. 2. Twins—Fiction. 3. Spies—Fiction.
4. Christian life—Fiction. 5. Mystery and detective stories.] I. Title. II. Series.
W72435Es   1996
[Fic]—dc20   96-15682
                                                                  CIP
                                                                  AC

96 97 98 99 00 01 02 03 — 10 9 8 7 6 5 4 3 2 1

He was lost in the icy wet darkness! Yet somewhere out there, only a few hundred yards away, glowed the lights that could bring him to safety. And somewhere in the same black night loomed his enemies!

But where? Justin kicked desperately in the water, not only to stay afloat, but to bring warmth back to his body. Caught in the trough between the long ocean swells, he saw nothing but rough, dark waves tossing and splashing all around him.

It had seemed so easy! His enemies hadn't followed his desperate dive overboard. The swim to land would be long and cold, but he was strong! He could make it! *But which way to swim?* He couldn't linger long in these winter waters!

A wave lifted him high. It held for just a moment, then curled over lazily, washing him under water. He choked and gagged as he fought his way back to the surface. But he had glimpsed the distant city skyline. Gritting his teeth to keep them from chattering, he struck out for the shore.

His arms and legs ached with cold. The swells grew higher and rougher and though he swam with all his strength the shoreline lights drew no closer.

I've got to keep going! he told himself grimly. If he didn't make it to safety his enemies would win. Unless the precious package tucked inside his jacket was returned safely, not only his family, but the entire country would be in danger!

As Justin swam on, a slow feeling of warmth crept into his

numbed limbs. He treaded water for a brief rest, letting swells lift and drop him in a sleepy rhythm. Why had he thought the waters so cold? This swim was almost pleasant—if only he wasn't so tired! His head drooped forward.

Wake up! Danger! He tried to ignore the screaming voice in his head. *You've got to keep moving!*

He forced himself into sluggish movement, scanning the night for light to guide him. But when he looked over his shoulder, he gasped in horror as a mountain of salt water curved slowly toward him.

He had to move, but his arms and legs felt like lead. For an instant, he watched the wave hover above him. Then gravity won as thousands of pounds of salt water crashed down upon him.

With dull surprise, Justin realized—*I'm drowning!*

chapter one

"Psst, Jenny! I think someone's following us!"

Jenny peered through a magnifying glass set in the top of a long, wooden case. Underneath was an ordinary pin, its tiny head etched with the entire Lord's Prayer. "What did you say?" she said absently without glancing up.

Justin's voice rose a little. "I said, I think someone's following us!"

This time Jenny did look up. "Oh, Justin!" she wailed. "Not again!"

Hands on her hips, she turned to survey the small trading post. Early November was long past tourist season on the Seattle waterfront, and the well-known Ye Olde Curiosity Shop, with souvenirs and oddities from all over the world, was almost empty of sightseers. Jenny's glance fell on two Middle Eastern men who were speaking Arabic next to a display of shrunken heads.

"Who, them?" she demanded. Eyeing the headdresses that topped the mens' American-style business suits, she giggled, "They look like shepherds in a Christmas play!"

"Not them!" Justin whispered with exasperation. He jerked his head across the room. "Him!"

Justin edged away from the glass case. Slipping behind an old player piano, he glanced out of the corner of his eye. Yes, there he was across the room! A stocky, middle-aged man with sandy hair!

Justin took a deep breath, running his fingers through short, carrot-hued curls. Then he peered around the side of the player piano. The sandy-haired man stood with his back to the Parker family. But Justin had felt the man's gaze on them—just as he had earlier that morning at the Firemen's Museum!

"Hey!" He whirled around, only to relax when he met his sister's frown.

"What are you acting so sneaky about?" she demanded. "You're not still thinking someone's following us!"

"Shhh! Not so loud!" Justin hissed. He dropped his voice to a whisper. "See that guy? It's the second time I've seen him this morning!"

Jenny hunched her shoulders, but at least she kept her voice down. "Oh, Justin, do you have to make a mystery out of everything? For once, let's just have some fun!"

"You're getting paranoid!" she added, now with irritation. "So a guy's exploring the wharf just like we are! That doesn't mean he's spying on us!"

Justin grinned suddenly. Maybe the guy thought *they* were following *him!* In any case, it was time he stopped looking for a mystery under every bush—or behind every player piano—and started enjoying this outing!

"Come on!" Jenny started down the aisle. "I want to try that slot machine."

They threaded their way past an assortment of polished rocks and a two-headed pig bottled in formaldehyde, stopping in front of an antique slot machine. Jenny dug into her jeans pockets. She held out a quarter and a penny. "You got another quarter?"

Justin dug a quarter out of his own pocket. His sister dropped them into an opening half way down the machine, then inserted the penny in the slot on top. It disappeared with a whirring sound. A moment later the machine spit out an egg-shaped piece of copper, now stamped with the words *Ye Olde Curiosity Shop*.

"I'll get it!" Both grabbed for the penny and bumped heads—hard! The stamped coin flew across the floor.

"Did you lose this?"

Justin blinked. A square face topped by thinning sandy hair swam into focus. He scrambled to his feet as he recognized the stocky, middle-aged man. He held out his hand. "Yeah, that's ours!"

The stocky stranger gave Justin a long, measured look before he dropped the engraved piece of copper into the boy's palm. His narrowed eyes were steel-grey, like the waters of Puget Sound. Justin shifted uneasily under the man's intent gaze. *Am I supposed to know this guy?*

He was sure he'd never seen this man before today. "Thanks!" he said, closing his fingers on the flattened penny.

"Any time!" With a pleasant nod, the sandy-haired man disappeared out the front door of the trading post.

Jenny got to her feet. She rubbed her forehead. "Boy, Justin, you've got a head as hard as a bowling ball!" But she forgot her sore head as their parents joined them and they filed outside.

"Where to now?" Dad demanded.

Jenny skidded to a stop under a brightly painted totem pole, her brown eyes sparking gold with excitement. She pushed back the dark curls a sea wind was tossing around her face. "Pike's Place Market! We haven't been there in a year!"

Dad groaned, running long fingers through his rusty, close-cropped hair. "Wouldn't you kids like to see the ships?" he suggested, but without much hope. "Pike's Place is much too far for an old man to climb!"

"Come on, Dad! You need some exercise!" Jenny poked her father on his flat stomach.

Justin glanced at his father's lean, freckled face. He *did* look tired.

Ron Parker worked long hours as a computer analyst consultant for Boeing, the airplane manufacturing company in Seattle, Washington. Just the day before, Dad had promised his family that his latest project was nearing an end and that the weekend belonged to them. When Saturday dawned clear and crisp, Justin and Jenny begged for this trip to the waterfront.

"All right!" Dad gave in. "But you'll have to carry me if I don't make it!"

Justin had forgotten about the many steep cement steps that rose from the wharf to Pike's Place Market. Pausing on a landing to catch his breath, he glanced idly back down the long stairway. The steps were empty except for one stocky, sandy-haired man who rested his elbows on the railing below.

Out of shape! Justin told himself, panting hard.

Pike's Place Market felt hot after the chill sea breeze of the waterfront. The strong smells of freshly caught seafood mingled with the smoke of burning incense and frying ethnic food. Justin drew in an appreciative breath. "Mmm. I'm hungry!"

"You're always hungry!" Jenny retorted. "Come on!"

"Look at the size of that salmon!" Justin licked his lips as a muscular youth tossed a silvery fish from his overflowing cart to the fish vendor behind the nearest counter. "I could eat the whole thing!"

Jenny peeped into a low, wooden case where a tangle of salt-water crabs snapped their pincers. Grinning, Justin shoved her toward the open box. Jenny let out a squawk and grabbed at the side of the case. Recovering her balance, she elbowed him sharply. "That wasn't funny!"

Mom and Dad caught up before Jenny could take revenge. The four Parkers threaded their way past the seafood to the vegetable and flower stalls.

Justin caught sight of the stocky stranger from Ye Olde Curiosity Shop fingering a leather belt two stalls away. The man cast a sideways glance at the Parkers. Justin frowned. Then, remembering his resolution, he changed the frown to a smile. "Hi, there!" he called with a cheerful wave. "I see you made it up okay!"

The sandy-haired man looked startled. But he waved before vanishing again.

Justin was starved by the time they made their way back down to the waterfront. Jenny poked him in the ribs as his stomach growled so loudly that a passing tourist stared. "Mom! Dad! We'd better feed Justin! He's embarrassing me!"

Stopping at one of the fast food stands that lined the wharf, Dad let them choose their favorites from the menu posted beside the counter. Even Justin had to agree that the generous helpings of breaded oysters, clams, scallops, and french fries should tide him over until suppertime.

They carried the heaping platters to a picnic area on the waterfront. Dad asked the blessing on the food, then glanced around the stone table. "Hey, guys," he demanded cheerfully, "where's the vinegar? We can't eat this without vinegar!"

Justin jumped to his feet. "I'll go get some."

Snatching a handful of fries, he hurried back to the seafood stand. He picked up the vinegar his father loved on fries and seafood, then started back. He had just reached the picnic area when a sudden glint of light caught the corner of his eye. Skidding to a stop, he stared!

The man with sandy hair sat at the far end of the picnic area. The noon sun reflected off the metallic trim of the binoculars he held tight against his eyes.

Him again! Justin's green eyes narrowed. He'd done like Jenny said! He'd tried to stop building a mystery out of every tourist who visited the same attractions as the Parkers. But those binoculars were a little too much for coincidence!

Justin hurried back to his own table. Sliding into his seat, he glanced across the picnic area. The table where the man sat was tucked behind a stone pillar. But now that he knew the stocky stranger was there, he could make out the tips of the binoculars sticking out.

Leaning over to his sister, he hissed, "Psst! Jenny!"

Jenny tossed a french fry to a seagull perched on the iron rail that ran along the edge of the wharf. The seagull dived, scooping up the treat in midair. "Did you say something?"

Justin jerked his head impatiently. "See that guy behind that pillar. That's the man from the Curiosity Shop!"

Jenny stared at the stone pillar. "So what?"

"Don't stare at him!" Justin hissed. "We don't want him to know *we* know he's there!" He lowered his voice. "See those binoculars? I told you he's following us!"

"All I see is a guy watching the boats!" Jenny waved a hand toward the rolling sea. She added, "And my brother making a fool of himself!"

"He *is* watching us!" Justin muttered stubbornly, but he didn't bring up the subject again.

The stranger was gone by the time the Parker's had finished eating. Dad stood up and stretched. "Ready to head home, kids?" he suggested hopefully.

"Home?" Jenny's heart-shaped face clouded over. "But you said we could go to Deer Island!"

"Did I say that?" Dad's reddish-brown eyebrows rose high. "You know my memory's been a little hazy lately."

Justin glanced at his watch. "The next ferry leaves in five minutes. We can catch it if we hurry."

"But I'm sure there was some business I had to take care of this afternoon!" His eyebrows knit together with concentration.

"Oh, now I remember!" Dad snapped his fingers and grinned. "That business *was* on Deer Island!"

"You didn't forget, Dad!" Jenny said reproachfully. "Now, stop teasing us! We're going to miss the ferry."

The Parkers reached the ferry dock just as the gangplank was being pulled in. Justin glanced back as he boarded, but if the stranger really had been following them, he was no longer anywhere in sight. Justin and Jenny hurried to the open prow of the ferry, leaving their parents to find seats in the enclosed passenger deck.

An icy sea breeze slapped Justin in the face, carrying with it the familiar tang of salt water. Pulling his jacket tight around his neck, he leaned over the rail. Far off to his left, the hump of Vashon Island rose evergreen above the waters of the Sound. Straight ahead was the far shore of Puget Sound and the nearer,

fast-approaching outline of the small island—now a state park—
that they called Deer Island.

The foghorn blasted as the ferry bumped gently against the
massive, wooden dock of the island. They hurried to join their
parents. Dad stopped at the bottom of the gangplank, one hand
shielding his eyes as he scanned the docks.

"He said he'd be here!" he muttered.

For the first time, Justin wondered what business his father
could have on the island. But Dad had already dropped his hand.
Striding rapidly along the boardwalk toward the clustered buildings of the ranger station, he called back, "Come on, you guys!
You wanted some exercise? So let's see who can beat me around
the island!"

Jenny giggled as a sleek yearling deer butted her gently. It was
from the herd of small deer released onto the island years before.
They were tame enough to be fed by hand.

Mom and Jenny opted to stay and feed the deer. But Dad and
Justin wandered down to the shore where a hiking trail had been
cut through the untrimmed brush and evergreen trees that
cloaked the island. It took them less than an hour to hike around
to the other side.

Justin stopped to study the shoreline. They were almost back
to the landing, and somewhere along in here was a hideout they
had found years earlier. It had been a long time since the Parkers
visited the island, but he was sure the place was somewhere
nearby. He had just spotted a familiar Santa-shaped stone when
he heard his father exclaim with relief, "There he is!"

Glancing up the bank, Justin's eyes widened at the strange figure moving up the trail from the landing. It was a man, he
realized, catching sight of a jutting, black beard. A man with
long, white robes and the same flowing headdress the Arab
tourists had worn in the Curiosity Shop. Dad hurried to meet
him. Grabbing him by the shoulders, the black-bearded stranger
kissed him on both cheeks.

Seattle's day for the Middle East! Justin grinned to himself.

Perched on a boulder at the water's edge, he watched as the two men walked slowly back down the trail, heads close together in earnest conversation.

It was the faint snap of a breaking twig that drew Justin's attention up the bank. He leaned forward with sudden interest. Yes, there it was! A flash of sandy-yellow among the evergreen branches overhanging the trail!

A man slipped into the shadow of a shaggy tamarack—a man Justin had already seen too often that day. And this time there could be no mistake about what the stranger was doing! The binoculars in his hands were trained on Dad and his companion.

What does this guy want with my family? Sliding down from the boulder, Justin started angrily up the bank. The man had no right to be following them around all day!

The intruder was too intent on watching the men up the trail to notice the boy circling quietly around behind him. Tapping him on the shoulder, Justin demanded, "Why are you spying on my father? You have no right to—"

But before he had finished speaking, the binoculars dropped, a hard hand clamped over his mouth, and Justin was being dragged helplessly into the tangle of underbrush!

chapter two

Wind-gnarled branches grabbed at Justin's jacket as the stranger dragged him through the underbrush. The sharp edges of the binoculars dug painfully into his back, and the hand clamped over his nose and mouth was slowly smothering him. All the warnings his parents had given him about men who preyed on children and teens swept through his mind.

Then he could breathe again! Still holding his hand lightly over Justin's mouth, his captor murmured in his ear, "Will you promise not to scream if I let you go?"

Justin managed a nod. Suddenly, he was free. Wiping the back of his hand across his mouth, he glanced around. He was in a small, grassy clearing closed in by bushes and stunted trees.

The boy looked sideways at his captor, tensing for a dash into the underbrush. But the sandy-haired man made no threatening moves. Instead, he leaned back against the trunk of a tree and crossed his arms. He sighed. "Well, kid! What am I supposed to do with you?"

The man shook his head. "I'll say this much! You have a sharp eye! None of the rest of your family even noticed me!"

Justin refused to be sidetracked by the man's compliment. "Who are you?" he demanded, his anger stiffened by the long rip he'd just discovered in his new winter jacket. "Why were you spying on us? And why did you drag me in here?"

"To keep you quiet!" Unfolding his arms, the stocky stranger straightened up from the tree. "You, boy, have just about man-aged to spoil an operation that's taken months to set up!"

Justin eyed his captor warily. This man didn't sound like a kidnapper. His square face was stern, and his voice had the crisp, authoritative tones of a man used to giving orders. "What operation? Are you a cop?"

The stranger gave Justin the same measured look he had given him in the Curiosity Shop. Justin shifted uncomfortably and glanced toward the underbrush. Maybe now was the time to make a break for freedom!

But before he could move, the man broke his silence. "You look like an intelligent young man," he said slowly. "And an honest one. I guess you deserve to know what you've stumbled into!"

He lifted his broad shoulders in a shrug. "I don't have much choice now, anyway! Not unless I'm prepared to silence you permanently!"

Justin drew in a sharp breath. The sandy-haired man thrust out an arm as he tensed to run. "Hey, kid! I was teasing!" The steel-grey eyes surveyed Justin thoughtfully. "Can I trust you to keep a secret?"

Justin hadn't seen any humor in the man's joke! He scowled, his freckled face hard with suspicion. "What kind of a secret?"

"A secret vital to the security of our country!" The stranger's tone was now sharp. "You asked if I'm a cop. I'm not! I'm a government agent. Do you know what that means, kid?"

Justin nodded, his eyes widening with sudden excitement. He'd read enough books and watched enough TV to know about secret government agents and spy operations! "You mean a secret agent? Like the CIA?"

He studied the stocky stranger with new respect. The man did look sort of like Justin's idea of a secret agent! The thin, straight line of his mouth gave his square features a grim look. Then there were those steel-grey eyes that saw everything!

Glancing up, Justin caught a look of amusement in the grey eyes. He flushed red as he realized how transparent his thoughts had been. Seeing his embarrassment, the stranger's shrewd gaze warmed to a sudden smile. It was a smile that completely transformed the square features, and Justin couldn't help grinning back. For the first time, he found himself relaxing.

"I really am a government agent!" the man said gently. Pulling out his wallet, he flipped it open to what looked like a badge. Justin caught the words *National Security Agency* before the man slapped the wallet shut and slipped it back into his pocket.

"My name is Grady O'Brian. I work for the National Security Agency. You could say we're related to the Central Intelligence Agency. At least we work together on occasion! But the CIA has operations all over the world. We worry only about threats to the security of our own country."

"You mean spies, and terrorists, and all that stuff?" Justin gave an understanding nod, then frowned. "But what does that have to do with us? Why are you following my dad? He's not a spy!"

The sandy-haired man didn't answer, and the thin line of his mouth was grim again. Justin's thoughts flickered back over the events of the day. A dozen news stories of the Middle East flashed through his mind as he suddenly remembered the Arabs in the Curiosity Shop and the mysterious, robed appearance of his father's companion.

"It's the Arabs, isn't it?" he burst out. "I'll bet that's it! They're one of those Muslim terrorist groups! That's why you followed us! You knew my dad was going to meet that Arab!"

"Shhh!" Grady O'Brian clapped a hand over Justin's mouth as his voice rose with excitement. He threw a cautious glance around the clearing. "Don't say that so loud!"

Letting go of Justin, O'Brian rubbed a hand across his face. "Look, kid, you've really put me in a difficult situation! First, you caught me trailing this man. Now you've figured out our entire operation. If you start talking around, you could ruin any chance we have of closing in on these terrorists! Do you understand what I'm saying?"

Justin understood all right! Everything he'd read had taught him how important complete secrecy was to a government operation. One small leak of information to the bad guys, and the good guys' entire plan would be blown!

"I won't tell anyone!" he promised quickly. He hesitated, then added, "Except...well, I should tell my Mom and Dad!"

"No!" Justin blinked at the explosive order.

"We can't afford the slightest risk of alerting the men we're after," Grady O'Brian said more quietly.

"If your mom and dad are like other parents, the first thing they'd do is get on the phone to check out your story. Your dad might even mention it to his Arab friend!"

The guy could be right! Justin admitted to himself. But aloud, he protested, "I don't keep secrets from my parents!"

"But this isn't your secret!" the sandy-haired man cut in sharply. "It's mine! Are you trying to tell me you've never kept a secret before? I'm sure your friends love it when you blab to your parents everything they tell you in confidence!"

"Of course I don't blab my friends' secrets!" Justin answered indignantly.

"So all I'm asking is that you do the same for me—keep a secret that's not yours to tell anyway! You just happened to stumble over something that's none of your business! And you'll be doing your country a big disfavor if you open your mouth about it!"

It wasn't quite the same, but Justin saw the government agent's point. He gave a reluctant nod. Grady patted him on the shoulder.

"Thanks, kid! Maybe someday you can impress everyone with today's adventures. But right now you just go on back to your family and forget this ever happened!"

Justin had no wish to hang around! He was already pushing into the underbrush when Grady O'Brian's call stopped him.

"Don't forget, kid!" There was no longer a smile in the steel-grey eyes. "Your country is counting on you to keep quiet! If this operation leaks out, we'll know who's responsible."

Neither Dad nor his Arab companion were in sight when Justin got back to the trail. He trotted down the path. Now that he had left the government agent behind, the whole adventure seemed a little unreal. But what a story it would have made to tell his friends!

He hadn't gone far when he saw Jenny hurrying up the trail to meet him. "Justin, where have you been? Dad's been looking all over for you!" Her brown eyes narrowed as she saw his torn jacket and scuffed jeans. "What happened to you?"

"Sorry, I can't tell you!" Justin's chest swelled with importance. He lowered his voice to a mysterious whisper. "It's a matter of national security!"

"Right!" Jenny answered scornfully. She broke into a run. "Come on! We're going to miss the ferry!"

When they arrived at the ferry dock, Mom and Dad were talking with a tall young man in a park ranger's uniform. "No, I'm alone here right now," the ranger said. "My boss and his wife are off to Hawaii for a month. Of course, there aren't many visitors in the winter."

Dad's eyebrows rose high as he caught sight of Justin. "Oh, there you are! Where did you disappear—"

The mournful bellow of the incoming ferry cut him off, to Justin's relief. They had crossed Puget Sound again and were driving home when Jenny leaned over the front seat of the car. "Hey, Dad! Who was that Arab guy you were talking to?"

"Who, Abdul?" Dad glanced into the rear view mirror. "Just a contact from work. He wanted to see me before leaving the country tonight."

"Deer Island sure seems a funny place for a business meeting!"

"That's your fault!" Dad grinned back at his daughter. "I told Abdul I'd already promised my family a day on the waterfront so we agreed to meet on Deer Island.

"Abdul el Kutub is an interesting man," Dad added, turning off the freeway into their own neighborhood. "I'll have to introduce you kids to him on his next trip. He's done a lot to improve Arab relations with the U.S."

That's what you think! Justin thought. Maybe someday he'd get a chance to tell his father about the mysterious Arab. He expected that Abdul el Kutub would be arrested for international terrorism.

He sat up straight as a sudden thought occurred to him. Did Grady O'Brian know that this Abdul was flying out of the country tonight? It would be awful if the terrorist escaped! If there was only some way to let the government agent know!

Catching a curious glance from his sister, Justin forced himself to relax against the seat. After all, the government had been tracking terrorists for a long time without his help! Besides, the sandy-haired agent had told Justin to forget the whole thing, and that's what he'd better do!

Tuesday evening, the whole family drove to Sea-Tac Airport to see off their best friend, Danny Nguyen, and his grandfather. Only a few weeks earlier, they had helped Danny and his grandfather bring about the arrest of the dreaded Dragon Tong that had been terrorizing the Vietnamese community. While the insurance company rebuilt the destroyed La Vie Restaurant, Mr. Nguyen was taking Danny on a long dreamed-of trip to his birthplace in Vietnam. Justin was sure going to miss his friend!

By Friday, Justin had nearly forgotten Grady O'Brian and the incident on Deer Island. School was out that day, so Dad had arranged for Justin to tour the prototype of Boeing's new 777 passenger plane.

It was almost noon when the engineering assistant showing Justin around the huge Boeing assembly plant dropped him off in front of the research facility where his father worked. Waving his thanks to the engineer, Justin pulled out the security pass his father had given him and started toward the wide, locked gate that led into the research complex. But he had taken only a few steps when he stopped short, his eyes widening.

The security guard, whose job it was to check everyone who went in and out of the research facility, was sitting in a guard box beside the gate. In front of the guard box, handing up a plastic-encased card through the open window, was a stocky, broad-shouldered figure he'd never expected to see again!

The government agent turned around in time to see Justin. Then Grady O'Brian snatched his plastic card from the security guard's hand and started toward Justin with long, rapid strides.

"What are you doing here, Gr—" Steel-strong fingers dug into Justin's upper arm, cutting off his exclamation.

"Be quiet, boy!" Grady hissed in Justin's ear.

"Hey, Justin!" The security guard leaned out of the window of the guard box. "Are you okay?"

Grady loosened his grip on Justin's arm, but he gave a warning shake of his head. Justin waved his free hand at the security guard. "Yeah, I'm fine!" he called weakly. "He's a friend!"

But as Grady hurried him down the sidewalk that ran along the high wall of the research facility, Justin demanded again, "What *are* you doing here? I thought you were supposed to be tailing that Arab guy!"

Grady didn't answer. He stopped beside a dark blue sedan parked just outside the front gate. Justin pulled hard against the man's steel grip. "Hey, I'm not going anywhere with you! I'm supposed to be meeting my dad!"

Opening the passenger door, Grady gave Justin a gentle

shove. "We're just going to have a little talk! Then I'll bring you back."

Justin didn't see any choice! Reluctantly, he climbed into the car. Justin heard a click as the car pulled away from the curb. He was locked in!

Justin was both angry and scared. Who was this man, really, and where was he taking him? Would he really bring him back? He glanced sideways. Grady whistled softly under his breath, his face thoughtful as he maneuvered in and out of traffic. But he offered no explanation!

Turning his back, Justin stared defiantly out the window. He made careful mental notes of each change of direction. If this man didn't keep his promise, he'd find his own way back!

After a few minutes Grady turned onto a wide street lined with tall, dingy apartment buildings. Pulling into an alley, Justin heard a click as the doors were unlocked. But Grady made no move to get out of the car. Instead, he turned to Justin.

"Look, kid, I'm sorry," he said. "I had to get you out of there before that guard started asking questions!"

"But, why?" A bewildered interest was beginning to replace Justin's anger. "I don't underst—"

"You'll get an explanation soon enough!" Grady cut in. He jerked his head toward the apartment building on the left. "Let's go!"

Taking hold of Justin's arm again, Grady guided him toward a side door in the apartment building. But this time his grip was loose. Inside, he pushed Justin ahead of him up a wooden staircase. When they had climbed two flights, he turned into a narrow, dimly lit hallway. Stopping in front of the last door on the right, he gave two rapid taps.

Grady didn't wait for an answer. Slipping a key into the lock, he pushed the door open. Justin, still unsure, stopped stubbornly in the doorway. He glanced around. The apartment was small and shabby with furniture that looked like rejects from a second-hand store. At the far end of the combination living room and kitchen, a door stood open leading into a tiny bedroom.

Across the room, a man sat hunched over a computer keyboard. Justin eyed the computer with admiration. He knew plenty about computers, and this had to be one of the most expensive and sophisticated Justin had ever seen.

Grady pushed Justin into the room. "Hacker, we've got a problem!" he said abruptly.

The man at the computer spun around in his chair. He was in his twenties with pale eyes and long, unwashed blonde hair tied in a ponytail. He gave Justin a long, unfriendly look. "What's the kid doing here?"

Giving Justin a gentle shove toward the sofa, Grady crossed the room to the computer desk.

Sitting on the sofa's edge, he watched the two men. Grady spoke in low, urgent tones. The younger man's sharp features grew sullen as he listened. Shaking his head angrily, he let out a violent curse.

"It isn't as bad as that!" Grady's low voice was firm. "I think the boy could be helpful!"

The two men glanced up suddenly. Catching Justin's interested gaze, Grady strode over to the front door and locked it. "It isn't that I don't trust you!" he told Justin, dropping the key into his pocket. "But we really do need to have that talk! You just stay put, and we'll be back in a moment!"

Grady gave a jerk of the head. With obvious reluctance, Hacker got to his feet and followed him into the bedroom. Ignoring Grady's order, Justin sprang to his feet as soon as the door closed behind the two men. He was trying the locked door when the two men returned. Grady's thin lips twitched as Justin dropped his hand guiltily from the knob, but he only motioned the boy back to the sofa.

Obeying, Justin glanced across the room. The ponytailed Hacker was already bent over the computer keyboard again. A computer hacker, he knew, was someone who was an expert at accessing computers. This man certainly deserved his nickname! His long, thin fingers flew across the keys.

Dropping into a nearby armchair, Grady gave Justin a thoughtful look. But Justin had had enough of waiting! Scooting forward to the edge of the sofa, he burst out belligerently, "So! Are you going to tell me why you're still following my dad around? If you really *were* a government agent, you'd know that Abdul el Kutub guy left the country a long time ago!"

"What did you say?" Grady leaned forward, his steel-grey eyes suddenly alert.

"I said that Abdul El Kutub guy already left the country!" Justin was puzzled by the sharpness of Grady's tone.

Grady relaxed back into his seat. "Of course, I know. I hadn't realized you were personally acquainted with the man," he said mildly.

"Oh, I'm not!" Justin assured him. "It was my dad who told me he was leaving the country!"

"Yes, we know that! Unfortunately, he'll be back!" The sandy-haired man broke off. After a moment's silence, he said slowly, "Justin, I'd hoped never to see you again! Unfortunately you decided to visit your father's office on the same day I chose to check out that facility. But maybe we can use this situation to both our advantage!"

"You know my name?" Justin was surprised.

"It's my job to know things. You'd be surprised what all I know about you and your family!" Grady smiled. Justin felt his suspicions ebbing, and he couldn't help grinning back. Uncertainly, he said, "Then...you really *are* a government agent!"

"Of course!" Grady said, still smiling. "But you're right to be cautious! I wish I could bring someone in to verify who I am, but that would jeopardize the security of this mission."

Taking out his wallet, Grady again flipped it open to the badge that read *National Security Agency* and handed it to Justin. He studied it closely. It sure looked authentic.

Handing back the wallet, he eyed the government agent.

There was something solid and completely trustworthy about the stocky figure and authoritative voice. Justin's tension ebbed away. He relaxed. "Yeah, I believe you!"

"Thank you!" Grady slid his wallet back into his pocket, then clasped his muscular fingers around one knee. "Justin, I'm going to do something right now that I've never done before. I'm going to have to give you classified information! I'll expect you to keep this information strictly in confidence!"

Justin perked up his ears. At last, he was going to find out what this was all about!

"For some time, certain highly classified military projects developed by Boeing have been falling into the hands of several very dangerous Middle East factions," Grady explained. "We finally traced the leak to Abdul el Kutub's regular visits to - Seattle."

"You mean, Abdul's been stealing government secrets and selling them to the Middle East?" Justin sat up straight. Then he frowned. "But…if you know it's Abdul, why don't you just arrest him? And what were you doing at my dad's research facility? Unless…of course!" He snapped his fingers. "You want to know who's giving him the information! It's got to be someone in the research department!"

Grady nodded approval. "That's right! Someone inside Boeing has been feeding information to Abdul. And now Abdul is offering the plans of a new classified military project to the highest Middle Eastern bidder! A project so new it hasn't even been finished!"

"What kind of a project?" Justin's eyes were wide with interest. This was better than a movie!

Grady was silent for a moment. Then he said, "Do you know what a radar detection system is, Justin?"

Justin nodded. He'd read about radar often enough in science magazines. Radar systems used radio waves to detect objects too far away to be seen.

"Then you know that modern armies have depended largely

on radar for locating and identifying hostile ships, planes, and missiles. That makes radar invisibility a big advantage in a war."

"You mean, like the F-117A Stealth Fighter!" Justin interrupted with excitement.

"Right!" Grady said with another approving nod. "Unfortunately, radar invisibility isn't enough anymore."

The scrape of a chair made Justin glance across the room. The ponytailed Hacker had swiveled away from his computer and was listening to Grady's explanation. Justin had the feeling that Hacker was amused. Turning back to Grady, Justin demanded, "So what does this have to do with my dad?"

"Everything! For years, your father's been working on a project they call an 'invisibility shield'—a screen that works equally well against radar detectors and long-range surveillance cameras. They weren't having much success until a recent breakthrough. Now the GP145—your father's project—is finally nearing completion."

The stocky agent leaned forward. "Think what that means, Justin! Military installations, aircraft, ships, even missiles completely invisible to enemy detection."

"Wow!" Justin grinned back, then added doubtfully, "So…is this project of my dad's the one Abdul is trying to sell?"

Grady's grin vanished. "Unfortunately, yes! If Abdul sold the GP145 to some Middle Eastern country, nothing we have could detect a missile equipped with that invisibility shield!"

Almost in a whisper, Justin answered, "They could blow up any part of the world they wanted!"

"You see why we can't just arrest Abdul." Grady's mouth was grim. "We *must* find out who at Boeing is leaking this classified data before it's too late! Before our traitor hands the invisibility shield over to Abdul el Kutub!"

"But why are you telling *me* all this?" Justin demanded, bewildered.

"Because I need your help!" Grady answered soberly. "You've certainly proved that you can be trusted!"

As Justin flushed with embarrassment and pleasure, he went on, "I was at Boeing this afternoon to get vital information. I ran the risk of alerting the traitor to our investigation. But if you can get the information we need, information to which your father has access, then no one at Boeing will know they are being investigated until it is too late!"

"You mean, you just want me to ask my dad to get you some information?" Justin said with relief. "Sure, I can do that! My dad would be glad to help!"

"No!" Justin looked at Grady in surprise. The agent shook his head. "No one in Boeing—certainly not your father—must know of this investigation! You'll have to get that information without telling him, or anyone else, what you've seen or heard here today!"

"Now, wait a minute!" Justin sat bolt upright, his freckled face indignant. "You asked me to keep your secret, and I did! But this is different! There's no way I'm going to spy on my own dad! I'm sorry, but you're just going to have to find someone else to get your information."

"I'm afraid you don't understand, Justin!" Grady's square features were suddenly stern. "This isn't a request—it's an order! And you will *not* say anything to your father or anyone else! Because if you don't cooperate, your father will immediately find himself under arrest for international espionage!"

Justin couldn't believe his ears! As Grady's words sank in, he jumped angrily to his feet. "What do you mean, you'll arrest my dad? Are you trying to say he's the spy?"

The steel-grey eyes were still cold. "Your father is one of the few people who has complete access to the plans and computer data. And you yourself saw him passing classified information to Abdul!"

Justin had a sudden horrifying mental picture of his father and Abdul el Kutub in earnest conversation on a lonely back trail of Deer Island. He pushed away the thought. Whatever the purpose of his father's meeting with Abdul, it had nothing to do with this!

"I don't believe it! I didn't see my dad pass anything to Abdul!" Justin started toward the door, his jaw thrust out with angry determination.

"I thought you would put the welfare of your country ahead of your own feelings!" Grady said sternly. "Your family will be in danger too if the GP145 falls into the wrong hands!"

Justin dropped his hand from the doorknob. "But I *know* my dad! He'd never *think* of selling government secrets."

"Justin, I believe you!" The kindness in Grady's voice startled Justin. *He's just doing his job!* he realized with astonishment. *He'd really like to help me!*

"I admit I didn't tell you everything the other day," Grady went on gently. "Yes, we've been following Abdul, but we've been following your father as well! His contacts with Abdul made him a suspect.

Grady pressed the tips of his muscular fingers together, his square features thoughtful. "No, I'm convinced your father isn't the one we want! I think someone else is using him to hand the computer disks over to Abdul. I'm sure your dad thinks he's passing along unclassified information."

"Well, I didn't see my dad passing any computer disks!" Justin said stubbornly. "And if you think he's innocent, why did you say you'd arrest—"

Grady cut him off with a sharp gesture. "The fact is that your father is the only one with access to the GP145 who has had *any* contact with Abdul! My superiors believe that your father is the traitor. They wanted me to pull him in when we caught him with Abdul last Saturday. But I convinced them that we needed more evidence."

With stern authority, he added, "You have no choice but to cooperate with me! The only way to get your father off the hook is to catch the real traitor. If we don't, your father will always be under suspicion of espionage. And if my superiors think they have enough evidence, they'll arrest him and send him to jail. By that time, the real traitor will have sold that invisibility shield to the highest bidder!"

"Then you've *got* to let me talk to my dad!" Justin jumped to his feet again. "If someone's really passing him those disks, I'm sure he can explain! You've *got* to let him prove he's innocent!"

"Justin, your father isn't the only one at stake here!" Grady said grimly. "The entire security of our country rests on our unmasking that spy! If the real traitor suspects that your father knows the truth about what's going on, he'll disappear. Ron Parker will have his chance to prove his innocence, but not until we've caught the real traitor!"

Justin wasn't completely convinced, but he nodded a reluctant agreement. "So what do you want me to do?"

"You can help by getting the information we need! First, we

need to know if your father could reproduce that invisibility shield himself if necessary. Then, we need to know exactly when the project will be finished. That's when Abdul and his accomplice will make their move. And we need to be waiting for them!"

"That shouldn't be too hard to find out," Justin admitted. He glanced back across the room. Hacker was hunched again over the computer. "Do you want me to call when I get the information?"

"Not directly, but you can use my beeper." Grady pulled out the small notebook he carried. Tearing out a sheet of paper, he scribbled numbers on it. "Here's my number. Page me when you've got the information, and I'll call back as soon as I can. Just don't show it to anyone. And don't use it unless you have to!"

Grady dropped Justin off a block short of the Boeing research facility. As he got out of the car, the agent reached over and patted him on the shoulder. "Don't look so gloomy, kid! We'll nail these guys!"

Grady's cheerful self-confidence didn't make Justin feel much better. After all, it wasn't *his* father who was being accused of international espionage! Glancing at his watch, Justin broke into a run.

But Dad was still in a meeting when he arrived out of breath at his father's third-floor office. Justin did his best to act natural when the meeting was over. But it wasn't easy, and as they drove home, he stared silently out the window.

"What's the matter, son?" Dad raised an eyebrow at Justin's preoccupied frown. "Didn't you like the tour?

Justin had totally forgotten the new Boeing 777. Sitting up straight, he forced a smile. "Sure, Dad! It was great! Thanks!"

He paused, then added, "You look awfully tired, Dad. I guess that project's really getting you down."

Dad ran a weary hand over his face. "Yes, I *am* tired! I'll be glad when the whole thing is done."

"But *when* will it be done?"

As soon as the words left his mouth, Justin knew he had spoken too urgently. Giving him a sharp look, Dad said, "I know I haven't had much time for you kids lately! Just hang in there a few more days!"

So it would be finished in just a few more days! Keeping his voice casual, Justin said, "I guess you're really important at Boeing, aren't you, Dad? I mean, for you to be in charge of an important project like that!"

Dad showed no suspicion of Justin's questions. "Where did you get the idea I was in charge of this project?" he asked now, glancing curiously across at Justin.

"You mean…you're not?" Justin sat up straight in astonishment. "But I thought it was your project."

"I'll take that as a compliment, son," Dad said with a chuckle. "No, I just head up the computer side of the project. The scientists and engineers are the ones who come up with the ideas and technical data for these projects."

"So you couldn't build one of your projects out of your head?" Justin tried not to sound too anxious. "Even after working on it all those months?"

Dad shook his head. "I don't think even a scientist could do that! There's just too much data involved. The scientists only know the part of the project they're working on. It takes the computers to put it all together." A sudden grin relaxed the tired lines of his mouth. "*And* computer analysts like me!"

Satisfied, Justin leaned back in his seat. This had been easier than he'd expected! But then, he thought with a twinge of guilt, Dad had no reason to hide anything from his son! Justin dismissed the thought firmly. After all, he was only doing this to help his father!

He punched in Grady's beeper number as soon as he got home. But though he lay awake until midnight, the government agent didn't call. Nor did he call the next day—or the next! Justin, who normally hated answering the phone, found himself jumping to his feet every time it rang.

"Expecting a girl to call?" Jenny teased.

Justin only grinned at her, but as two more days went by, he grew restless and irritable. Dad was now working until midnight or later every night, and on two nights he didn't come home at all.

On Wednesday, Justin flunked the first test of his school career—a science test, at that! But he barely glanced at the grade before stuffing it into his backpack. Why hadn't Grady called if he needed that information so urgently?

But that very evening Grady finally called. "It's for you, Justin!" Mom announced. "Some man!"

"I'll take it in the office," Justin said. Catching his sister's curious glance, he added quickly, "It's probably my science teacher! You know, that test I flunked!"

Justin dashed downstairs to his mother's basement office. Locking the door behind him, he grabbed the phone and said, "I've been trying to reach you for days!"

Grady's crisp tones were hurried and tired. "Is it finished?"

Justin shook his head. "No, I don't think so, but it could be any day! Dad didn't even come home last night! That's always a sign they're almost finished."

"I've got to have that information as soon as possible!" Grady said sharply. "Every hour counts!"

Justin only said, "I'll call when I find out. And about my dad…"

He repeated all his father had told him about the project. "So my dad doesn't know how to build that invisibility shield!" he finished eagerly. "That proves he's innocent, doesn't it?"

There was a silence on the other end of the line. Grady's voice sounded strange when he finally spoke. "Justin, your father is listed as one of the few men with access to the entire project! Are you telling me he's only a computer hacker?"

Justin found himself repeating his father's words. "The scientists couldn't build the thing without the computer analysts to put all their data together!"

"So the computer's the only one who knows everything about the project!" Grady sounded far away as though he were talking to himself or someone else in the room. Then his voice warmed with approval. "Thanks, Justin! You've done your country a great service!"

Hanging up the phone, Justin unlocked the office door. Jenny was waiting right outside. "Since when is the science teacher a man?" she demanded. "And why did you lock the office door?"

The sound of the front door opening saved him from answering.

Justin followed Jenny upstairs. By the time they reached the living room, Dad had already dropped his briefcase onto a chair and was pulling off his tie. His eyes were rimmed with red and he rubbed a weary hand over two days of beard stubble. "What a marathon! But we all voted to push on until we had finished."

Justin drew in a sharp breath. Jenny asked eagerly, "You mean the project's finished? Can you tell us now what you were working on? Is it still a secret?"

"Yes, Jenny, it's finished! Right down to the very last data entry!"

Justin edged toward the hall. If only Grady had called just half an hour later! As he hurried downstairs, he heard his father say, "No, Jenny, I'm afraid the project's still classified!"

Justin lay awake far into the night. He'd punched in Grady's beeper number, but the government agent didn't call back.

Grady still hadn't called by the time they headed for the bus stop the next morning. He had to do something soon! If he waited for Grady to call, it might be too late to save his dad's project.

Jenny realized that her brother was daydreaming again. Planting herself right in front of him, she demanded, "What's with you, Justin! You're acting like a zombie!"

When she repeated her question, he shrugged. "I didn't get much sleep last night."

Jenny looked skeptical. "Or maybe it's that science teacher that called? Come on, tell me! Who was it, really?"

Stretching his long legs into a run, he called over his shoulder, "We'd better hurry or we'll miss the bus!"

Jenny gave her brother a funny look when she noticed the bus wasn't even in sight yet. But Justin had made up his mind. Grady had to have that information even if he had to deliver it in person!

Once on the bus, Jenny didn't ask any more awkward questions. He knew she hadn't forgotten the phone call, but at least she'd decided to let the matter drop!

When they got to school, Justin checked his schedule. He had two study halls right before lunch, and the monitor never noticed if anyone sneaked out. He was sure he could find Grady's apartment and still be back for science.

Before the final bell had finished ringing, he was out the door. His plan couldn't have gone smoother! A city bus pulled up, heading in the direction that Grady had taken him.

The bus dropped him off in the low-income neighborhood where Grady had taken him the week before. But not even the slow rain that trickled down the neck of his jacket dampened his growing excitement.

Boy, is Grady going to be glad to see me! Justin trotted down an alley, shoulders hunched against the cold. He glanced at his watch. It was later than he thought—almost noon. He'd have to hurry if he was going to make it back to school before he was missed.

Finding one apartment among all these shabby, brick buildings wasn't going to be easy. In the drizzle and mist, they all looked the same.

Then he caught sight of a dark blue sedan in front of an apartment complex. That had to be Grady's car!

He hurried down the street until he reached the blue sedan.

TWIN PURSUITS

ESCAPE
to Deer Island

JEANETTE WINDLE

ESCAPE TO DEER ISLAND

published by Multnomah Books
a part of the Questar publishing family

© 1996 by JEANETTE WINDLE

International Standard Book Number: 0-88070-906-5

Cover illustration by xxx

Printed in the United States of America.

For information:
QUESTAR PUBLISHERS, INC.
POST OFFICE BOX 1720
SISTERS, OREGON 97759

Library of Congress Cataloging-in-Publication Data:

Windle, Jeanette.
    Escape to Deer Island / by Jeanette Windle.
        p. cm. — (Twin pursuits)
    Summary: After a mysterious man suggests that their father may be selling infor-
mation to a Middle Eastern terrorist, the twins become entangled in international
espionage.
    ISBN 0-88070-906-5 (alk. paper)
    [1. Robbers and outlaws—Fiction. 2. Twins—Fiction. 3. Spies—Fiction.
4. Christian life—Fiction. 5. Mystery and detective stories.] I. Title. II. Series.
W72435Es   1996
[Fic]—dc20   96-15682
                                                                     CIP
                                                                     AC

96 97 98 99 00 01 02 03 — 10 9 8 7 6 5 4 3 2 1

He was lost in the icy wet darkness! Yet somewhere out there, only a few hundred yards away, glowed the lights that could bring him to safety. And somewhere in the same black night loomed his enemies!

But where? Justin kicked desperately in the water, not only to stay afloat, but to bring warmth back to his body. Caught in the trough between the long ocean swells, he saw nothing but rough, dark waves tossing and splashing all around him.

It had seemed so easy! His enemies hadn't followed his desperate dive overboard. The swim to land would be long and cold, but he was strong! He could make it! *But which way to swim?* He couldn't linger long in these winter waters!

A wave lifted him high. It held for just a moment, then curled over lazily, washing him under water. He choked and gagged as he fought his way back to the surface. But he had glimpsed the distant city skyline. Gritting his teeth to keep them from chattering, he struck out for the shore.

His arms and legs ached with cold. The swells grew higher and rougher and though he swam with all his strength the shoreline lights drew no closer.

I've got to keep going! he told himself grimly. If he didn't make it to safety his enemies would win. Unless the precious package tucked inside his jacket was returned safely, not only his family, but the entire country would be in danger!

As Justin swam on, a slow feeling of warmth crept into his

numbed limbs. He treaded water for a brief rest, letting swells lift and drop him in a sleepy rhythm. Why had he thought the waters so cold? This swim was almost pleasant—if only he wasn't so tired! His head drooped forward.

Wake up! Danger! He tried to ignore the screaming voice in his head. *You've got to keep moving!*

He forced himself into sluggish movement, scanning the night for light to guide him. But when he looked over his shoulder, he gasped in horror as a mountain of salt water curved slowly toward him.

He had to move, but his arms and legs felt like lead. For an instant, he watched the wave hover above him. Then gravity won as thousands of pounds of salt water crashed down upon him.

With dull surprise, Justin realized—*I'm drowning!*

chapter one

"Psst, Jenny! I think someone's following us!"

Jenny peered through a magnifying glass set in the top of a long, wooden case. Underneath was an ordinary pin, its tiny head etched with the entire Lord's Prayer. "What did you say?" she said absently without glancing up.

Justin's voice rose a little. "I said, I think someone's following us!"

This time Jenny did look up. "Oh, Justin!" she wailed. "Not again!"

Hands on her hips, she turned to survey the small trading post. Early November was long past tourist season on the Seattle waterfront, and the well-known Ye Olde Curiosity Shop, with souvenirs and oddities from all over the world, was almost empty of sightseers. Jenny's glance fell on two Middle Eastern men who were speaking Arabic next to a display of shrunken heads.

"Who, them?" she demanded. Eyeing the headdresses that topped the mens' American-style business suits, she giggled, "They look like shepherds in a Christmas play!"

"Not them!" Justin whispered with exasperation. He jerked his head across the room. "Him!"

Justin edged away from the glass case. Slipping behind an old player piano, he glanced out of the corner of his eye. Yes, there he was across the room! A stocky, middle-aged man with sandy hair!

Justin took a deep breath, running his fingers through short, carrot-hued curls. Then he peered around the side of the player piano. The sandy-haired man stood with his back to the Parker family. But Justin had felt the man's gaze on them—just as he had earlier that morning at the Firemen's Museum!

"Hey!" He whirled around, only to relax when he met his sister's frown.

"What are you acting so sneaky about?" she demanded. "You're not still thinking someone's following us!"

"Shhh! Not so loud!" Justin hissed. He dropped his voice to a whisper. "See that guy? It's the second time I've seen him this morning!"

Jenny hunched her shoulders, but at least she kept her voice down. "Oh, Justin, do you have to make a mystery out of everything? For once, let's just have some fun!"

"You're getting paranoid!" she added, now with irritation. "So a guy's exploring the wharf just like we are! That doesn't mean he's spying on us!"

Justin grinned suddenly. Maybe the guy thought *they* were following *him!* In any case, it was time he stopped looking for a mystery under every bush—or behind every player piano—and started enjoying this outing!

"Come on!" Jenny started down the aisle. "I want to try that slot machine."

They threaded their way past an assortment of polished rocks and a two-headed pig bottled in formaldehyde, stopping in front of an antique slot machine. Jenny dug into her jeans pockets. She held out a quarter and a penny. "You got another quarter?"

Justin dug a quarter out of his own pocket. His sister dropped them into an opening half way down the machine, then inserted the penny in the slot on top. It disappeared with a whirring sound. A moment later the machine spit out an egg-shaped piece of copper, now stamped with the words *Ye Olde Curiosity Shop.*

"I'll get it!" Both grabbed for the penny and bumped heads—hard! The stamped coin flew across the floor.

"Did you lose this?"

Justin blinked. A square face topped by thinning sandy hair swam into focus. He scrambled to his feet as he recognized the stocky, middle-aged man. He held out his hand. "Yeah, that's ours!"

The stocky stranger gave Justin a long, measured look before he dropped the engraved piece of copper into the boy's palm. His narrowed eyes were steel-grey, like the waters of Puget Sound. Justin shifted uneasily under the man's intent gaze. *Am I supposed to know this guy?*

He was sure he'd never seen this man before today. "Thanks!" he said, closing his fingers on the flattened penny.

"Any time!" With a pleasant nod, the sandy-haired man disappeared out the front door of the trading post.

Jenny got to her feet. She rubbed her forehead. "Boy, Justin, you've got a head as hard as a bowling ball!" But she forgot her sore head as their parents joined them and they filed outside.

"Where to now?" Dad demanded.

Jenny skidded to a stop under a brightly painted totem pole, her brown eyes sparking gold with excitement. She pushed back the dark curls a sea wind was tossing around her face. "Pike's Place Market! We haven't been there in a year!"

Dad groaned, running long fingers through his rusty, close-cropped hair. "Wouldn't you kids like to see the ships?" he suggested, but without much hope. "Pike's Place is much too far for an old man to climb!"

"Come on, Dad! You need some exercise!" Jenny poked her father on his flat stomach.

Justin glanced at his father's lean, freckled face. He *did* look tired.

Ron Parker worked long hours as a computer analyst consultant for Boeing, the airplane manufacturing company in Seattle, Washington. Just the day before, Dad had promised his family that his latest project was nearing an end and that the weekend belonged to them. When Saturday dawned clear and crisp, Justin and Jenny begged for this trip to the waterfront.

"All right!" Dad gave in. "But you'll have to carry me if I don't make it!"

Justin had forgotten about the many steep cement steps that rose from the wharf to Pike's Place Market. Pausing on a landing to catch his breath, he glanced idly back down the long stairway. The steps were empty except for one stocky, sandy-haired man who rested his elbows on the railing below.

Out of shape! Justin told himself, panting hard.

Pike's Place Market felt hot after the chill sea breeze of the waterfront. The strong smells of freshly caught seafood mingled with the smoke of burning incense and frying ethnic food. Justin drew in an appreciative breath. "Mmm. I'm hungry!"

"You're always hungry!" Jenny retorted. "Come on!"

"Look at the size of that salmon!" Justin licked his lips as a muscular youth tossed a silvery fish from his overflowing cart to the fish vendor behind the nearest counter. "I could eat the whole thing!"

Jenny peeped into a low, wooden case where a tangle of salt-water crabs snapped their pincers. Grinning, Justin shoved her toward the open box. Jenny let out a squawk and grabbed at the side of the case. Recovering her balance, she elbowed him sharply. "That wasn't funny!"

Mom and Dad caught up before Jenny could take revenge. The four Parkers threaded their way past the seafood to the vegetable and flower stalls.

Justin caught sight of the stocky stranger from Ye Olde Curiosity Shop fingering a leather belt two stalls away. The man cast a sideways glance at the Parkers. Justin frowned. Then, remembering his resolution, he changed the frown to a smile. "Hi, there!" he called with a cheerful wave. "I see you made it up okay!"

The sandy-haired man looked startled. But he waved before vanishing again.

Justin was starved by the time they made their way back down to the waterfront. Jenny poked him in the ribs as his stomach growled so loudly that a passing tourist stared. "Mom! Dad! We'd better feed Justin! He's embarrassing me!"

Stopping at one of the fast food stands that lined the wharf, Dad let them choose their favorites from the menu posted beside the counter. Even Justin had to agree that the generous helpings of breaded oysters, clams, scallops, and french fries should tide him over until suppertime.

They carried the heaping platters to a picnic area on the waterfront. Dad asked the blessing on the food, then glanced around the stone table. "Hey, guys," he demanded cheerfully, "where's the vinegar? We can't eat this without vinegar!"

Justin jumped to his feet. "I'll go get some."

Snatching a handful of fries, he hurried back to the seafood stand. He picked up the vinegar his father loved on fries and seafood, then started back. He had just reached the picnic area when a sudden glint of light caught the corner of his eye. Skidding to a stop, he stared!

The man with sandy hair sat at the far end of the picnic area. The noon sun reflected off the metallic trim of the binoculars he held tight against his eyes.

Him again! Justin's green eyes narrowed. He'd done like Jenny said! He'd tried to stop building a mystery out of every tourist who visited the same attractions as the Parkers. But those binoculars were a little too much for coincidence!

Justin hurried back to his own table. Sliding into his seat, he glanced across the picnic area. The table where the man sat was tucked behind a stone pillar. But now that he knew the stocky stranger was there, he could make out the tips of the binoculars sticking out.

Leaning over to his sister, he hissed, "Psst! Jenny!"

Jenny tossed a french fry to a seagull perched on the iron rail that ran along the edge of the wharf. The seagull dived, scooping up the treat in midair. "Did you say something?"

Justin jerked his head impatiently. "See that guy behind that pillar. That's the man from the Curiosity Shop!"

Jenny stared at the stone pillar. "So what?"

"Don't stare at him!" Justin hissed. "We don't want him to know *we* know he's there!" He lowered his voice. "See those binoculars? I told you he's following us!"

"All I see is a guy watching the boats!" Jenny waved a hand toward the rolling sea. She added, "And my brother making a fool of himself!"

"He *is* watching us!" Justin muttered stubbornly, but he didn't bring up the subject again.

The stranger was gone by the time the Parker's had finished eating. Dad stood up and stretched. "Ready to head home, kids?" he suggested hopefully.

"Home?" Jenny's heart-shaped face clouded over. "But you said we could go to Deer Island!"

"Did I say that?" Dad's reddish-brown eyebrows rose high. "You know my memory's been a little hazy lately."

Justin glanced at his watch. "The next ferry leaves in five minutes. We can catch it if we hurry."

"But I'm sure there was some business I had to take care of this afternoon!" His eyebrows knit together with concentration.

"Oh, now I remember!" Dad snapped his fingers and grinned. "That business *was* on Deer Island!"

"You didn't forget, Dad!" Jenny said reproachfully. "Now, stop teasing us! We're going to miss the ferry."

The Parkers reached the ferry dock just as the gangplank was being pulled in. Justin glanced back as he boarded, but if the stranger really had been following them, he was no longer anywhere in sight. Justin and Jenny hurried to the open prow of the ferry, leaving their parents to find seats in the enclosed passenger deck.

An icy sea breeze slapped Justin in the face, carrying with it the familiar tang of salt water. Pulling his jacket tight around his neck, he leaned over the rail. Far off to his left, the hump of Vashon Island rose evergreen above the waters of the Sound. Straight ahead was the far shore of Puget Sound and the nearer, fast-approaching outline of the small island—now a state park—that they called Deer Island.

The foghorn blasted as the ferry bumped gently against the massive, wooden dock of the island. They hurried to join their parents. Dad stopped at the bottom of the gangplank, one hand shielding his eyes as he scanned the docks.

"He said he'd be here!" he muttered.

For the first time, Justin wondered what business his father could have on the island. But Dad had already dropped his hand. Striding rapidly along the boardwalk toward the clustered buildings of the ranger station, he called back, "Come on, you guys! You wanted some exercise? So let's see who can beat me around the island!"

Jenny giggled as a sleek yearling deer butted her gently. It was from the herd of small deer released onto the island years before. They were tame enough to be fed by hand.

Mom and Jenny opted to stay and feed the deer. But Dad and Justin wandered down to the shore where a hiking trail had been cut through the untrimmed brush and evergreen trees that cloaked the island. It took them less than an hour to hike around to the other side.

Justin stopped to study the shoreline. They were almost back to the landing, and somewhere along in here was a hideout they had found years earlier. It had been a long time since the Parkers visited the island, but he was sure the place was somewhere nearby. He had just spotted a familiar Santa-shaped stone when he heard his father exclaim with relief, "There he is!"

Glancing up the bank, Justin's eyes widened at the strange figure moving up the trail from the landing. It was a man, he realized, catching sight of a jutting, black beard. A man with long, white robes and the same flowing headdress the Arab tourists had worn in the Curiosity Shop. Dad hurried to meet him. Grabbing him by the shoulders, the black-bearded stranger kissed him on both cheeks.

Seattle's day for the Middle East! Justin grinned to himself.

Perched on a boulder at the water's edge, he watched as the two men walked slowly back down the trail, heads close together in earnest conversation.

It was the faint snap of a breaking twig that drew Justin's attention up the bank. He leaned forward with sudden interest. Yes, there it was! A flash of sandy-yellow among the evergreen branches overhanging the trail!

A man slipped into the shadow of a shaggy tamarack—a man Justin had already seen too often that day. And this time there could be no mistake about what the stranger was doing! The binoculars in his hands were trained on Dad and his companion.

What does this guy want with my family? Sliding down from the boulder, Justin started angrily up the bank. The man had no right to be following them around all day!

The intruder was too intent on watching the men up the trail to notice the boy circling quietly around behind him. Tapping him on the shoulder, Justin demanded, "Why are you spying on my father? You have no right to—"

But before he had finished speaking, the binoculars dropped, a hard hand clamped over his mouth, and Justin was being dragged helplessly into the tangle of underbrush!

Wind-gnarled branches grabbed at Justin's jacket as the stranger dragged him through the underbrush. The sharp edges of the binoculars dug painfully into his back, and the hand clamped over his nose and mouth was slowly smothering him. All the warnings his parents had given him about men who preyed on children and teens swept through his mind.

Then he could breathe again! Still holding his hand lightly over Justin's mouth, his captor murmured in his ear, "Will you promise not to scream if I let you go?"

Justin managed a nod. Suddenly, he was free. Wiping the back of his hand across his mouth, he glanced around. He was in a small, grassy clearing closed in by bushes and stunted trees.

The boy looked sideways at his captor, tensing for a dash into the underbrush. But the sandy-haired man made no threatening moves. Instead, he leaned back against the trunk of a tree and crossed his arms. He sighed. "Well, kid! What am I supposed to do with you?"

The man shook his head. "I'll say this much! You have a sharp eye! None of the rest of your family even noticed me!"

Justin refused to be sidetracked by the man's compliment. "Who are you?" he demanded, his anger stiffened by the long rip he'd just discovered in his new winter jacket. "Why were you spying on us? And why did you drag me in here?"

"To keep you quiet!" Unfolding his arms, the stocky stranger

straightened up from the tree. "You, boy, have just about managed to spoil an operation that's taken months to set up!"

Justin eyed his captor warily. This man didn't sound like a
kidnapper. His square face was stern, and his voice had the crisp,
authoritative tones of a man used to giving orders. "What operation? Are you a cop?"

The stranger gave Justin the same measured look he had
given him in the Curiosity Shop. Justin shifted uncomfortably
and glanced toward the underbrush. Maybe now was the time to
make a break for freedom!

But before he could move, the man broke his silence. "You
look like an intelligent young man," he said slowly. "And an honest one. I guess you deserve to know what you've stumbled into!"

He lifted his broad shoulders in a shrug. "I don't have much
choice now, anyway! Not unless I'm prepared to silence you permanently!"

Justin drew in a sharp breath. The sandy-haired man thrust
out an arm as he tensed to run. "Hey, kid! I was teasing!" The
steel-grey eyes surveyed Justin thoughtfully. "Can I trust you to
keep a secret?"

Justin hadn't seen any humor in the man's joke! He scowled,
his freckled face hard with suspicion. "What kind of a secret?"

"A secret vital to the security of our country!" The stranger's
tone was now sharp. "You asked if I'm a cop. I'm not! I'm a government agent. Do you know what that means, kid?"

Justin nodded, his eyes widening with sudden excitement.
He'd read enough books and watched enough TV to know about
secret government agents and spy operations! "You mean a secret
agent? Like the CIA?"

He studied the stocky stranger with new respect. The man
did look sort of like Justin's idea of a secret agent! The thin,
straight line of his mouth gave his square features a grim look.
Then there were those steel-grey eyes that saw everything!

Glancing up, Justin caught a look of amusement in the grey
eyes. He flushed red as he realized how transparent his thoughts

had been. Seeing his embarrassment, the stranger's shrewd gaze warmed to a sudden smile. It was a smile that completely transformed the square features, and Justin couldn't help grinning back. For the first time, he found himself relaxing.

"I really am a government agent!" the man said gently. Pulling out his wallet, he flipped it open to what looked like a badge. Justin caught the words *National Security Agency* before the man slapped the wallet shut and slipped it back into his pocket.

"My name is Grady O'Brian. I work for the National Security Agency. You could say we're related to the Central Intelligence Agency. At least we work together on occasion! But the CIA has operations all over the world. We worry only about threats to the security of our own country."

"You mean spies, and terrorists, and all that stuff?" Justin gave an understanding nod, then frowned. "But what does that have to do with us? Why are you following my dad? He's not a spy!"

The sandy-haired man didn't answer, and the thin line of his mouth was grim again. Justin's thoughts flickered back over the events of the day. A dozen news stories of the Middle East flashed through his mind as he suddenly remembered the Arabs in the Curiosity Shop and the mysterious, robed appearance of his father's companion.

"It's the Arabs, isn't it?" he burst out. "I'll bet that's it! They're one of those Muslim terrorist groups! That's why you followed us! You knew my dad was going to meet that Arab!"

"Shhh!" Grady O'Brian clapped a hand over Justin's mouth as his voice rose with excitement. He threw a cautious glance around the clearing. "Don't say that so loud!"

Letting go of Justin, O'Brian rubbed a hand across his face. "Look, kid, you've really put me in a difficult situation! First, you caught me trailing this man. Now you've figured out our entire operation. If you start talking around, you could ruin any chance we have of closing in on these terrorists! Do you understand what I'm saying?"

Justin understood all right! Everything he'd read had taught him how important complete secrecy was to a government operation. One small leak of information to the bad guys, and the good guys' entire plan would be blown!

"I won't tell anyone!" he promised quickly. He hesitated, then added, "Except…well, I should tell my Mom and Dad!"

"No!" Justin blinked at the explosive order.

"We can't afford the slightest risk of alerting the men we're after," Grady O'Brian said more quietly.

"If your mom and dad are like other parents, the first thing they'd do is get on the phone to check out your story. Your dad might even mention it to his Arab friend!"

The guy could be right! Justin admitted to himself. But aloud, he protested, "I don't keep secrets from my parents!"

"But this isn't your secret!" the sandy-haired man cut in sharply. "It's mine! Are you trying to tell me you've never kept a secret before? I'm sure your friends love it when you blab to your parents everything they tell you in confidence!"

"Of course I don't blab my friends' secrets!" Justin answered indignantly.

"So all I'm asking is that you do the same for me—keep a secret that's not yours to tell anyway! You just happened to stumble over something that's none of your business! And you'll be doing your country a big disfavor if you open your mouth about it!"

It wasn't quite the same, but Justin saw the government agent's point. He gave a reluctant nod. Grady patted him on the shoulder.

"Thanks, kid! Maybe someday you can impress everyone with today's adventures. But right now you just go on back to your family and forget this ever happened!"

Justin had no wish to hang around! He was already pushing into the underbrush when Grady O'Brian's call stopped him.

"Don't forget, kid!" There was no longer a smile in the steel-grey eyes. "Your country is counting on you to keep quiet! If this operation leaks out, we'll know who's responsible."

Neither Dad nor his Arab companion were in sight when Justin got back to the trail. He trotted down the path. Now that he had left the government agent behind, the whole adventure seemed a little unreal. But what a story it would have made to tell his friends!

He hadn't gone far when he saw Jenny hurrying up the trail to meet him. "Justin, where have you been? Dad's been looking all over for you!" Her brown eyes narrowed as she saw his torn jacket and scuffed jeans. "What happened to you?"

"Sorry, I can't tell you!" Justin's chest swelled with importance. He lowered his voice to a mysterious whisper. "It's a matter of national security!"

"Right!" Jenny answered scornfully. She broke into a run. "Come on! We're going to miss the ferry!"

When they arrived at the ferry dock, Mom and Dad were talking with a tall young man in a park ranger's uniform. "No, I'm alone here right now," the ranger said. "My boss and his wife are off to Hawaii for a month. Of course, there aren't many visitors in the winter."

Dad's eyebrows rose high as he caught sight of Justin. "Oh, there you are! Where did you disappear—"

The mournful bellow of the incoming ferry cut him off, to Justin's relief. They had crossed Puget Sound again and were driving home when Jenny leaned over the front seat of the car. "Hey, Dad! Who was that Arab guy you were talking to?"

"Who, Abdul?" Dad glanced into the rear view mirror. "Just a contact from work. He wanted to see me before leaving the country tonight."

"Deer Island sure seems a funny place for a business meeting!"

"That's your fault!" Dad grinned back at his daughter. "I told Abdul I'd already promised my family a day on the waterfront so we agreed to meet on Deer Island.

"Abdul el Kutub is an interesting man," Dad added, turning off the freeway into their own neighborhood. "I'll have to introduce you kids to him on his next trip. He's done a lot to improve Arab relations with the U.S."

That's what you think! Justin thought. Maybe someday he'd get a chance to tell his father about the mysterious Arab. He expected that Abdul el Kutub would be arrested for international terrorism.

He sat up straight as a sudden thought occurred to him. Did Grady O'Brian know that this Abdul was flying out of the country tonight? It would be awful if the terrorist escaped! If there was only some way to let the government agent know!

Catching a curious glance from his sister, Justin forced himself to relax against the seat. After all, the government had been tracking terrorists for a long time without his help! Besides, the sandy-haired agent had told Justin to forget the whole thing, and that's what he'd better do!

Tuesday evening, the whole family drove to Sea-Tac Airport to see off their best friend, Danny Nguyen, and his grandfather. Only a few weeks earlier, they had helped Danny and his grandfather bring about the arrest of the dreaded Dragon Tong that had been terrorizing the Vietnamese community. While the insurance company rebuilt the destroyed La Vie Restaurant, Mr. Nguyen was taking Danny on a long dreamed-of trip to his birthplace in Vietnam. Justin was sure going to miss his friend!

By Friday, Justin had nearly forgotten Grady O'Brian and the incident on Deer Island. School was out that day, so Dad had arranged for Justin to tour the prototype of Boeing's new 777 passenger plane.

It was almost noon when the engineering assistant showing Justin around the huge Boeing assembly plant dropped him off in front of the research facility where his father worked. Waving his thanks to the engineer, Justin pulled out the security pass his father had given him and started toward the wide, locked gate that led into the research complex. But he had taken only a few steps when he stopped short, his eyes widening.

The security guard, whose job it was to check everyone who went in and out of the research facility, was sitting in a guard box beside the gate. In front of the guard box, handing up a plastic-encased card through the open window, was a stocky, broad-shouldered figure he'd never expected to see again!

The government agent turned around in time to see Justin. Then Grady O'Brian snatched his plastic card from the security guard's hand and started toward Justin with long, rapid strides.

"What are you doing here, Gr—" Steel-strong fingers dug into Justin's upper arm, cutting off his exclamation.

"Be quiet, boy!" Grady hissed in Justin's ear.

"Hey, Justin!" The security guard leaned out of the window of the guard box. "Are you okay?"

Grady loosened his grip on Justin's arm, but he gave a warning shake of his head. Justin waved his free hand at the security guard. "Yeah, I'm fine!" he called weakly. "He's a friend!"

But as Grady hurried him down the sidewalk that ran along the high wall of the research facility, Justin demanded again, "What *are* you doing here? I thought you were supposed to be tailing that Arab guy!"

Grady didn't answer. He stopped beside a dark blue sedan parked just outside the front gate. Justin pulled hard against the man's steel grip. "Hey, I'm not going anywhere with you! I'm supposed to be meeting my dad!"

Opening the passenger door, Grady gave Justin a gentle

shove. "We're just going to have a little talk! Then I'll bring you back."

Justin didn't see any choice! Reluctantly, he climbed into the car. Justin heard a click as the car pulled away from the curb. He was locked in!

Justin was both angry and scared. Who was this man, really, and where was he taking him? Would he really bring him back? He glanced sideways. Grady whistled softly under his breath, his face thoughtful as he maneuvered in and out of traffic. But he offered no explanation!

Turning his back, Justin stared defiantly out the window. He made careful mental notes of each change of direction. If this man didn't keep his promise, he'd find his own way back!

After a few minutes Grady turned onto a wide street lined with tall, dingy apartment buildings. Pulling into an alley, Justin heard a click as the doors were unlocked. But Grady made no move to get out of the car. Instead, he turned to Justin.

"Look, kid, I'm sorry," he said. "I had to get you out of there before that guard started asking questions!"

"But, why?" A bewildered interest was beginning to replace Justin's anger. "I don't underst—"

"You'll get an explanation soon enough!" Grady cut in. He jerked his head toward the apartment building on the left. "Let's go!"

Taking hold of Justin's arm again, Grady guided him toward a side door in the apartment building. But this time his grip was loose. Inside, he pushed Justin ahead of him up a wooden staircase. When they had climbed two flights, he turned into a narrow, dimly lit hallway. Stopping in front of the last door on the right, he gave two rapid taps.

Grady didn't wait for an answer. Slipping a key into the lock, he pushed the door open. Justin, still unsure, stopped stubbornly in the doorway. He glanced around. The apartment was small and shabby with furniture that looked like rejects from a second-hand store. At the far end of the combination living room and kitchen, a door stood open leading into a tiny bedroom.

Across the room, a man sat hunched over a computer keyboard. Justin eyed the computer with admiration. He knew plenty about computers, and this had to be one of the most expensive and sophisticated Justin had ever seen.

Grady pushed Justin into the room. "Hacker, we've got a problem!" he said abruptly.

The man at the computer spun around in his chair. He was in his twenties with pale eyes and long, unwashed blonde hair tied in a ponytail. He gave Justin a long, unfriendly look. "What's the kid doing here?"

Giving Justin a gentle shove toward the sofa, Grady crossed the room to the computer desk.

Sitting on the sofa's edge, he watched the two men. Grady spoke in low, urgent tones. The younger man's sharp features grew sullen as he listened. Shaking his head angrily, he let out a violent curse.

"It isn't as bad as that!" Grady's low voice was firm. "I think the boy could be helpful!"

The two men glanced up suddenly. Catching Justin's interested gaze, Grady strode over to the front door and locked it. "It isn't that I don't trust you!" he told Justin, dropping the key into his pocket. "But we really do need to have that talk! You just stay put, and we'll be back in a moment!"

Grady gave a jerk of the head. With obvious reluctance, Hacker got to his feet and followed him into the bedroom. Ignoring Grady's order, Justin sprang to his feet as soon as the door closed behind the two men. He was trying the locked door when the two men returned. Grady's thin lips twitched as Justin dropped his hand guiltily from the knob, but he only motioned the boy back to the sofa.

Obeying, Justin glanced across the room. The ponytailed Hacker was already bent over the computer keyboard again. A computer hacker, he knew, was someone who was an expert at accessing computers. This man certainly deserved his nickname! His long, thin fingers flew across the keys.

Dropping into a nearby armchair, Grady gave Justin a thoughtful look. But Justin had had enough of waiting! Scooting forward to the edge of the sofa, he burst out belligerently, "So! Are you going to tell me why you're still following my dad around? If you really *were* a government agent, you'd know that Abdul el Kutub guy left the country a long time ago!"

"What did you say?" Grady leaned forward, his steel-grey eyes suddenly alert.

"I said that Abdul El Kutub guy already left the country!" Justin was puzzled by the sharpness of Grady's tone.

Grady relaxed back into his seat. "Of course, I know. I hadn't realized you were personally acquainted with the man," he said mildly.

"Oh, I'm not!" Justin assured him. "It was my dad who told me he was leaving the country!"

"Yes, we know that! Unfortunately, he'll be back!" The sandy-haired man broke off. After a moment's silence, he said slowly, "Justin, I'd hoped never to see you again! Unfortunately you decided to visit your father's office on the same day I chose to check out that facility. But maybe we can use this situation to both our advantage!"

"You know my name?" Justin was surprised.

"It's my job to know things. You'd be surprised what all I know about you and your family!" Grady smiled. Justin felt his suspicions ebbing, and he couldn't help grinning back. Uncertainly, he said, "Then…you really *are* a government agent!"

"Of course!" Grady said, still smiling. "But you're right to be cautious! I wish I could bring someone in to verify who I am, but that would jeopardize the security of this mission."

Taking out his wallet, Grady again flipped it open to the badge that read *National Security Agency* and handed it to Justin. He studied it closely. It sure looked authentic.

Handing back the wallet, he eyed the government agent.

There was something solid and completely trustworthy about the stocky figure and authoritative voice. Justin's tension ebbed away. He relaxed. "Yeah, I believe you!"

"Thank you!" Grady slid his wallet back into his pocket, then clasped his muscular fingers around one knee. "Justin, I'm going to do something right now that I've never done before. I'm going to have to give you classified information! I'll expect you to keep this information strictly in confidence!"

Justin perked up his ears. At last, he was going to find out what this was all about!

"For some time, certain highly classified military projects developed by Boeing have been falling into the hands of several very dangerous Middle East factions," Grady explained. "We finally traced the leak to Abdul el Kutub's regular visits to - Seattle."

"You mean, Abdul's been stealing government secrets and selling them to the Middle East?" Justin sat up straight. Then he frowned. "But…if you know it's Abdul, why don't you just arrest him? And what were you doing at my dad's research facility? Unless…of course!" He snapped his fingers. "You want to know who's giving him the information! It's got to be someone in the research department!"

Grady nodded approval. "That's right! Someone inside Boeing has been feeding information to Abdul. And now Abdul is offering the plans of a new classified military project to the highest Middle Eastern bidder! A project so new it hasn't even been finished!"

"What kind of a project?" Justin's eyes were wide with interest. This was better than a movie!

Grady was silent for a moment. Then he said, "Do you know what a radar detection system is, Justin?"

Justin nodded. He'd read about radar often enough in science magazines. Radar systems used radio waves to detect objects too far away to be seen.

"Then you know that modern armies have depended largely

on radar for locating and identifying hostile ships, planes, and missiles. That makes radar invisibility a big advantage in a war."

"You mean, like the F-117A Stealth Fighter!" Justin interrupted with excitement.

"Right!" Grady said with another approving nod. "Unfortunately, radar invisibility isn't enough anymore."

The scrape of a chair made Justin glance across the room. The ponytailed Hacker had swiveled away from his computer and was listening to Grady's explanation. Justin had the feeling that Hacker was amused. Turning back to Grady, Justin demanded, "So what does this have to do with my dad?"

"Everything! For years, your father's been working on a project they call an 'invisibility shield'—a screen that works equally well against radar detectors and long-range surveillance cameras. They weren't having much success until a recent breakthrough. Now the GP145—your father's project—is finally nearing completion."

The stocky agent leaned forward. "Think what that means, Justin! Military installations, aircraft, ships, even missiles completely invisible to enemy detection."

"Wow!" Justin grinned back, then added doubtfully, "So…is this project of my dad's the one Abdul is trying to sell?"

Grady's grin vanished. "Unfortunately, yes! If Abdul sold the GP145 to some Middle Eastern country, nothing we have could detect a missile equipped with that invisibility shield!"

Almost in a whisper, Justin answered, "They could blow up any part of the world they wanted!"

"You see why we can't just arrest Abdul." Grady's mouth was grim. "We *must* find out who at Boeing is leaking this classified data before it's too late! Before our traitor hands the invisibility shield over to Abdul el Kutub!"

"But why are you telling *me* all this?" Justin demanded, bewildered.

"Because I need your help!" Grady answered soberly. "You've certainly proved that you can be trusted!"

As Justin flushed with embarrassment and pleasure, he went on, "I was at Boeing this afternoon to get vital information. I ran the risk of alerting the traitor to our investigation. But if you can get the information we need, information to which your father has access, then no one at Boeing will know they are being investigated until it is too late!"

"You mean, you just want me to ask my dad to get you some information?" Justin said with relief. "Sure, I can do that! My dad would be glad to help!"

"No!" Justin looked at Grady in surprise. The agent shook his head. "No one in Boeing—certainly not your father—must know of this investigation! You'll have to get that information without telling him, or anyone else, what you've seen or heard here today!"

"Now, wait a minute!" Justin sat bolt upright, his freckled face indignant. "You asked me to keep your secret, and I did! But this is different! There's no way I'm going to spy on my own dad! I'm sorry, but you're just going to have to find someone else to get your information."

"I'm afraid you don't understand, Justin!" Grady's square features were suddenly stern. "This isn't a request—it's an order! And you will *not* say anything to your father or anyone else! Because if you don't cooperate, your father will immediately find himself under arrest for international espionage!"

chapter four

Justin couldn't believe his ears! As Grady's words sank in, he jumped angrily to his feet. "What do you mean, you'll arrest my dad? Are you trying to say he's the spy?"

The steel-grey eyes were still cold. "Your father is one of the few people who has complete access to the plans and computer data. And you yourself saw him passing classified information to Abdul!"

Justin had a sudden horrifying mental picture of his father and Abdul el Kutub in earnest conversation on a lonely back trail of Deer Island. He pushed away the thought. Whatever the purpose of his father's meeting with Abdul, it had nothing to do with this!

"I don't believe it! I didn't see my dad pass anything to Abdul!" Justin started toward the door, his jaw thrust out with angry determination.

"I thought you would put the welfare of your country ahead of your own feelings!" Grady said sternly. "Your family will be in danger too if the GP145 falls into the wrong hands!"

Justin dropped his hand from the doorknob. "But I *know* my dad! He'd never *think* of selling government secrets."

"Justin, I believe you!" The kindness in Grady's voice startled Justin. *He's just doing his job!* he realized with astonishment. *He'd really like to help me!*

"I admit I didn't tell you everything the other day," Grady went on gently. "Yes, we've been following Abdul, but we've been following your father as well! His contacts with Abdul made him a suspect.

Grady pressed the tips of his muscular fingers together, his square features thoughtful. "No, I'm convinced your father isn't the one we want! I think someone else is using him to hand the computer disks over to Abdul. I'm sure your dad thinks he's passing along unclassified information."

"Well, I didn't see my dad passing any computer disks!" Justin said stubbornly. "And if you think he's innocent, why did you say you'd arrest—"

Grady cut him off with a sharp gesture. "The fact is that your father is the only one with access to the GP145 who has had *any* contact with Abdul! My superiors believe that your father is the traitor. They wanted me to pull him in when we caught him with Abdul last Saturday. But I convinced them that we needed more evidence."

With stern authority, he added, "You have no choice but to cooperate with me! The only way to get your father off the hook is to catch the real traitor. If we don't, your father will always be under suspicion of espionage. And if my superiors think they have enough evidence, they'll arrest him and send him to jail. By that time, the real traitor will have sold that invisibility shield to the highest bidder!"

"Then you've *got* to let me talk to my dad!" Justin jumped to his feet again. "If someone's really passing him those disks, I'm sure he can explain! You've *got* to let him prove he's innocent!"

"Justin, your father isn't the only one at stake here!" Grady said grimly. "The entire security of our country rests on our unmasking that spy! If the real traitor suspects that your father knows the truth about what's going on, he'll disappear. Ron Parker will have his chance to prove his innocence, but not until we've caught the real traitor!"

Justin wasn't completely convinced, but he nodded a reluctant agreement. "So what do you want me to do?"

"You can help by getting the information we need! First, we

need to know if your father could reproduce that invisibility shield himself if necessary. Then, we need to know exactly when the project will be finished. That's when Abdul and his accomplice will make their move. And we need to be waiting for them!"

"That shouldn't be too hard to find out," Justin admitted. He glanced back across the room. Hacker was hunched again over the computer. "Do you want me to call when I get the information?"

"Not directly, but you can use my beeper." Grady pulled out the small notebook he carried. Tearing out a sheet of paper, he scribbled numbers on it. "Here's my number. Page me when you've got the information, and I'll call back as soon as I can. Just don't show it to anyone. And don't use it unless you have to!"

Grady dropped Justin off a block short of the Boeing research facility. As he got out of the car, the agent reached over and patted him on the shoulder. "Don't look so gloomy, kid! We'll nail these guys!"

Grady's cheerful self-confidence didn't make Justin feel much better. After all, it wasn't *his* father who was being accused of international espionage! Glancing at his watch, Justin broke into a run.

But Dad was still in a meeting when he arrived out of breath at his father's third-floor office. Justin did his best to act natural when the meeting was over. But it wasn't easy, and as they drove home, he stared silently out the window.

"What's the matter, son?" Dad raised an eyebrow at Justin's preoccupied frown. "Didn't you like the tour?

Justin had totally forgotten the new Boeing 777. Sitting up straight, he forced a smile. "Sure, Dad! It was great! Thanks!"

He paused, then added, "You look awfully tired, Dad. I guess that project's really getting you down."

Dad ran a weary hand over his face. "Yes, I *am* tired! I'll be glad when the whole thing is done."

"But *when* will it be done?"

As soon as the words left his mouth, Justin knew he had spoken too urgently. Giving him a sharp look, Dad said, "I know I haven't had much time for you kids lately! Just hang in there a few more days!"

So it would be finished in just a few more days! Keeping his voice casual, Justin said, "I guess you're really important at Boeing, aren't you, Dad? I mean, for you to be in charge of an important project like that!"

Dad showed no suspicion of Justin's questions. "Where did you get the idea I was in charge of this project?" he asked now, glancing curiously across at Justin.

"You mean…you're not?" Justin sat up straight in astonishment. "But I thought it was your project."

"I'll take that as a compliment, son," Dad said with a chuckle. "No, I just head up the computer side of the project. The scientists and engineers are the ones who come up with the ideas and technical data for these projects."

"So you couldn't build one of your projects out of your head?" Justin tried not to sound too anxious. "Even after working on it all those months?"

Dad shook his head. "I don't think even a scientist could do that! There's just too much data involved. The scientists only know the part of the project they're working on. It takes the computers to put it all together." A sudden grin relaxed the tired lines of his mouth. "*And* computer analysts like me!"

Satisfied, Justin leaned back in his seat. This had been easier than he'd expected! But then, he thought with a twinge of guilt, Dad had no reason to hide anything from his son! Justin dismissed the thought firmly. After all, he was only doing this to help his father!

He punched in Grady's beeper number as soon as he got home. But though he lay awake until midnight, the government agent didn't call. Nor did he call the next day—or the next! Justin, who normally hated answering the phone, found himself jumping to his feet every time it rang.

"Expecting a girl to call?" Jenny teased.

Justin only grinned at her, but as two more days went by, he grew restless and irritable. Dad was now working until midnight or later every night, and on two nights he didn't come home at all.

On Wednesday, Justin flunked the first test of his school career—a science test, at that! But he barely glanced at the grade before stuffing it into his backpack. Why hadn't Grady called if he needed that information so urgently?

But that very evening Grady finally called. "It's for you, Justin!" Mom announced. "Some man!"

"I'll take it in the office," Justin said. Catching his sister's curious glance, he added quickly, "It's probably my science teacher! You know, that test I flunked!"

Justin dashed downstairs to his mother's basement office. Locking the door behind him, he grabbed the phone and said, "I've been trying to reach you for days!"

Grady's crisp tones were hurried and tired. "Is it finished?"

Justin shook his head. "No, I don't think so, but it could be any day! Dad didn't even come home last night! That's always a sign they're almost finished."

"I've got to have that information as soon as possible!" Grady said sharply. "Every hour counts!"

Justin only said, "I'll call when I find out. And about my dad…"

He repeated all his father had told him about the project. "So my dad doesn't know how to build that invisibility shield!" he finished eagerly. "That proves he's innocent, doesn't it?"

There was a silence on the other end of the line. Grady's voice sounded strange when he finally spoke. "Justin, your father is listed as one of the few men with access to the entire project! Are you telling me he's only a computer hacker?"

Justin found himself repeating his father's words. "The scientists couldn't build the thing without the computer analysts to put all their data together!"

"So the computer's the only one who knows everything about the project!" Grady sounded far away as though he were talking to himself or someone else in the room. Then his voice warmed with approval. "Thanks, Justin! You've done your country a great service!"

Hanging up the phone, Justin unlocked the office door. Jenny was waiting right outside. "Since when is the science teacher a man?" she demanded. "And why did you lock the office door?"

The sound of the front door opening saved him from answering.

Justin followed Jenny upstairs. By the time they reached the living room, Dad had already dropped his briefcase onto a chair and was pulling off his tie. His eyes were rimmed with red and he rubbed a weary hand over two days of beard stubble. "What a marathon! But we all voted to push on until we had finished."

Justin drew in a sharp breath. Jenny asked eagerly, "You mean the project's finished? Can you tell us now what you were working on? Is it still a secret?"

"Yes, Jenny, it's finished! Right down to the very last data entry!"

Justin edged toward the hall. If only Grady had called just half an hour later! As he hurried downstairs, he heard his father say, "No, Jenny, I'm afraid the project's still classified!"

Justin lay awake far into the night. He'd punched in Grady's beeper number, but the government agent didn't call back.

Grady still hadn't called by the time they headed for the bus stop the next morning. He had to do something soon! If he waited for Grady to call, it might be too late to save his dad's project.

Jenny realized that her brother was daydreaming again. Planting herself right in front of him, she demanded, "What's with you, Justin! You're acting like a zombie!"

When she repeated her question, he shrugged. "I didn't get much sleep last night."

Jenny looked skeptical. "Or maybe it's that science teacher that called? Come on, tell me! Who was it, really?"

Stretching his long legs into a run, he called over his shoulder, "We'd better hurry or we'll miss the bus!"

Jenny gave her brother a funny look when she noticed the bus wasn't even in sight yet. But Justin had made up his mind. Grady had to have that information even if he had to deliver it in person!

Once on the bus, Jenny didn't ask any more awkward questions. He knew she hadn't forgotten the phone call, but at least she'd decided to let the matter drop!

When they got to school, Justin checked his schedule. He had two study halls right before lunch, and the monitor never noticed if anyone sneaked out. He was sure he could find Grady's apartment and still be back for science.

Before the final bell had finished ringing, he was out the door. His plan couldn't have gone smoother! A city bus pulled up, heading in the direction that Grady had taken him.

The bus dropped him off in the low-income neighborhood where Grady had taken him the week before. But not even the slow rain that trickled down the neck of his jacket dampened his growing excitement.

Boy, is Grady going to be glad to see me! Justin trotted down an alley, shoulders hunched against the cold. He glanced at his watch. It was later than he thought—almost noon. He'd have to hurry if he was going to make it back to school before he was missed.

Finding one apartment among all these shabby, brick buildings wasn't going to be easy. In the drizzle and mist, they all looked the same.

Then he caught sight of a dark blue sedan in front of an apartment complex. That had to be Grady's car!

He hurried down the street until he reached the blue sedan.

plans from the mainframe computer data banks. And the computer records every addition, deletion, or copy made of a file."

Grady nodded toward the blue disk. "That disk holds a special program Hacker has made up. It'll check the data banks for any unauthorized copies of computer files. The program can tell us exactly which office terminal and which password has been used to get in the data banks. That should give us a lead on our traitor!"

Uh, oh! A program that checked the computer log for unauthorized copies? Justin remembered his father handing a computer disk to Abdul.

"Uh, Grady," he said hesitantly. "What if there isn't any traitor in Boeing? What if Abdul's been getting that stuff from someone innocent?"

Hacker gave a short bark of laughter. "What's the matter, kid?" he sneered. "Worried that your father isn't so innocent, after all?"

"Of course not!" Justin retorted. "It's just that I've met the people my dad works with! They all seem like pretty nice guys!"

Grady looked down at Justin. "Look, kid! If you can get the GP145 file for us before Abdul or someone else manages to destroy it, I'll guarantee the NSA will forget about your father— whether he's innocent or not!"

Justin nodded, then Grady clapped him on the back. "By tonight everything will be all over, and Abdul will be in custody. But first we need you to get us a copy of that file! If not for your country, then do it for your father!"

"But what about my dad?" he protested, accepting with reluctance the pouch Hacker shoved into his hands. "He'll be in the office!"

"No problem!" Grady picked up the phone. "I'll make a call that will get him out of his office for an hour or two. You just think of a good excuse to get in there!"

The government agent began punching in numbers. Shoving the black pouch inside his jacket, Justin wandered across the room and looked out the window. The brown van was still sitting across the street.

"Hey, Grady!" he called. "That man in the brown van. Who is he? And why is following me instead of my dad?"

"What man?" Slamming down the phone, Grady strode rapidly to Justin's side.

"*That* man!" Justin pointed out as the driver walked around to the back of the van.

The driver opened the back doors of the van and four men climbed out of the back. The five men walked toward the apartment building.

Justin's voice faltered. "You mean…isn't he working for you? But I saw him coming out of this building!"

Yanking open the drawers of the desk, the government agent began stuffing papers into a small briefcase. "Hacker, they've found us! Clear that computer!"

Glancing at the screen, Justin saw that Hacker was deleting file after file from the computer. Not even bothering to switch off the computer, Hacker started toward the door. Grady grabbed the briefcase in one hand and Justin's arm in the other. "Let's get out of here!"

But it was too late! Already, Justin heard the sound of running feet in the hall. A moment later, a hard fist pounded at the apartment door!

The two men looked at each other. Then, as though they'd exchanged a signal, they turned on their heels and headed for the bedroom, Grady herding Justin ahead of him.

Grady locked the bedroom door, propping a chair under the doorknob. Hacker was already scrambling out the window. Throwing a leg over the sill, Justin followed him onto a rusty fire escape. Behind him, he could hear shouts and heavy blows on the apartment door. Grady was climbing out when Justin heard a crash. The front door!

"Who are those guys?" Justin found breath to ask as they clattered down the fire stairs. "Do they work for Abdul?"

"Yes!" Grady's square features were grim. "And they're after me, not you or your dad. I don't know how they found me, but they're not likely to be too pleasant if they catch up to us!"

Justin heard another crash. Abdul's men were in the bedroom! Justin quickened his pace, taking the rusty, metal stairs two and three at a time. He had just reached the alley when he heard the faint scrape of a window being raised.

Justin had wondered why the agent parked his car in such an out-of-the-way spot. Now he knew! He danced with impatience as Grady unlocked the sedan. Already he could hear a clattering on the metal staircase above him.

Grady yanked open the back car door. Hacker climbed into the passenger side. "Get in and keep that red hair of yours down!" he ordered crisply.

But it was too late for that! Justin was tumbling into the back seat when a voice shouted, "Hey, that's the Parker kid!" Glancing up, he saw a man leaning over the metal banister one flight above. He had a gun!

The van driver clattered downstairs with two of his men at his heels. But Grady had wasted no time! By the time the three men reached the ground, the sedan was racing out of the alley.

Justin, kneeling on the back seat, saw the van driver drop to a crouch behind them. His eyes widened in alarm as the man raised his gun to aim at the back of the sedan. But before Justin could even duck, the van driver lowered his weapon. Waving for the others to follow, he ran after the sedan.

But the car was already rounding the front of the building, tires screeching around the corner. Grady sped down the long, straight street that ran between the dingy brick buildings of the housing development. Justin watched the five men sprint for the brown van. By then the sedan was turning another corner.

Grady didn't slow down once they'd left the van behind. "I think we've lost them!" he called back after a few minutes. "Okay, Justin! Tell me exactly where and when you've seen those men before!"

Justin quickly filled in the government agent on the few times he'd seen the brown van. At any instant, he expected to hear the wail of a police siren behind him.

"Good job, kid!" Grady commented when he finished. "I guess that's another one we owe you!"

"Uh, boss!" Hacker was looking into his side view mirror. "We've got trouble coming!"

Justin swiveled around to look out the back window. The brown van was about a block behind them.

Grady glanced into his rear view mirror. "Just hold on! We're almost there!"

Putting on a burst of speed, he swerved to the right into the outer lane of traffic. Just a few yards ahead was a freeway entrance. Justin let out a whoop of triumph as he saw the brown van swept in the flow of traffic. "You've got 'em! They're gone!"

"They'll be back!" Grady said. Maneuvering onto the freeway, he crossed all six lanes of traffic in one continuous move. Justin's palms showed little half-moons where his nails had dug in, but his green eyes glowed with admiration and excitement. This was beginning to look like a high-speed chase in an action movie!

Grady sped down the first off ramp and turned onto a street. Slowing down, he looked back at Justin.

"Okay, Justin, here's the plan! Jump out as soon as I stop. Get over to Boeing and get those files. Your father should be out for a couple of hours. I'll call you when I can."

Justin nodded. He slid a hand into his jacket. In all the excitement, he'd actually forgotten what had started all this chase! But the black pouch was still there. He scooted over to the door.

Grady slowed as they came to a major intersection. "Go!"

Justin was out of the car even before it had stopped. Darting across to the sidewalk, he ducked behind a parked car. Back where they had turned off the freeway, a brown van was nosing into traffic.

The dark blue sedan peeled off with a squeal of tires. Justin crouched behind the parked car until the van sped by. Straightening up, he stared anxiously after the two speeding vehicles. What if those men caught up to Grady and Hacker?

He pushed the thought out of his mind. Grady was a professional. He could shake those guys! In the meantime, he had his own job to do. He broke into a run, not slowing down until he came to a bus stop. A half-hour later, he was at the gates of the Boeing research facility.

Justin didn't have the security pass Dad always gave him when he visited his office, and his one worry had been how he was to get past the strict security at the front gate. But the security guard on duty was one he had met several times before. It was, in fact, the same guard who had been there the day he toured the prototype for the new Boeing 777.

"Hey, Charlie!" Justin called up. "Is my dad still here? You know, Ron Parker? Can I get through to his office?"

"Hi, Justin!" The guard cracked open the window of the guard box. "I'm afraid you missed your dad! He left almost an hour ago."

"Great!" Justin's exclamation brought a strange look from the guard, and he added hurriedly, "I don't want my dad to know I'm here. It's a surprise."

"Oh?" Charlie gave Justin a broad wink. "Someone's birthday coming up, I'll bet!"

The gate creaked open. "Make it quick!" he called down. "You really shouldn't be in here without a security pass."

"Hey, Justin! Wait!" Charlie called him back with a frantic wave of the hand. Justin skidded to an impatient stop. But his eyes brightened when he saw the small, plastic tag the security guard was holding out to him.

"So no one'll give you any hassle!" Charlie told him with a grin. "Just don't let them get a look at my ugly mug on the front!"

Justin clipped the security pass to the front of his jacket. Waving his thanks, he broke into a run. If his father had been gone almost an hour, he might not have much time left!

The security guard in the front lobby was the usual day guard Justin had seen every time he visited his father's office. Stopping a few feet away, Justin called out a greeting and tapped his security pass. The guard waved him on by. Before he walked to his father's office Justin leaned over the counter and hissed, "Hey, Mr. Wu! If my dad comes, please don't tell him I'm here. It's a surprise!"

With a grunt of consent, the security guard went back to his surveillance monitors. Justin headed for the research wing. He passed several lab technicians in white coats on the way, but none cast more than a casual glance at his security badge. This was even easier than he'd hoped!

His father's office was halfway down a long corridor of identical doors. He knocked. A cheerful voice called, "Come in!"

Dad's secretary looked up from her desk as Justin stepped

into the room. She was a plump, middle-aged woman with a pleasant face and glasses that were continually sliding down her nose. "Why, Justin! What are *you* doing here?"

"Hi, Miss Pettigrew! Is my dad in?" Justin stole a quick glance around the office.

"No, I'm afraid Mr. Parker was called out unexpectedly." Miss Pettigrew's plucked eyebrows arched high. "He didn't say you'd be in this morning, Justin. Aren't you supposed to be in school?"

"He didn't know I was coming," Justin admitted. Remembering the first guard's assumption, he added with a conspiratorial whisper, "It's a surprise! You know—that special day coming up!"

He didn't dare elaborate as his dad's secretary knew every birthday and anniversary in the family. But Miss Pettigrew was not by nature an inquisitive person. She glanced back at her computer screen with a touch of impatience.

Justin leaned over her desk. "Did Dad say where he was going? And when he'll be back?"

Miss Pettigrew let out a quiet sigh. Pushing up her glasses, she brought her attention back to Justin. "He didn't say much of anything! Some man called about an hour ago. Some emergency to do with that latest project of his!"

So Grady had gotten Dad out of the way! Justin glanced at his watch. Dad would be back as soon as he found out Grady's 'emergency' didn't really exist. He'd have to hurry! He crossed quickly to the door behind Miss Pettigrew's desk. "I'll wait for him in his office."

"Good idea!" Miss Pettigrew said crisply. But she smiled at him as she turned back to her computer screen.

Shutting the office door behind him, Justin crossed the thick carpeting to his father's desk. He slid into his father's office chair. Pulling out the black pouch Hacker had given him, he turned his attention to the computer terminal in front of him.

Then, consulting Hacker's instructions, he typed in the first of a series of words and numbers. The sequence made no sense to him, but he obeyed all instructions until heavy, red letters spelled

MENU in the middle of the screen. Below was a short, numbered list. Justin ran down the list until he reached the words *Government Projects.* Justin clicked the mouse until the screen filled with a much longer list of computer files.

The words *CLASSIFIED. PASSWORD ACCESS REQUIRED* blinked ominously at the top of the computer screen. But the list of files below gave no hint of their top secret contents. Instead of some exotic code name, each file was indicated only by the letters GP followed by a number. Consulting Hacker's list of instructions again, Justin moved the mouse to *GP145* and clicked once. The list disappeared. The simple instruction *Type password* appeared at the top of the screen.

Justin wiped his sweaty hands on his jeans. Now was the test of his boast to Grady. But he knew the last event of any importance in the Parker household: Mom's birthday and the unveiling of the new office just one month before on Wednesday, October 11.

He calculated rapidly in his head. Reducing the date to numbers, he reversed their order, and multiplied the number by two. Then he carefully typed *1 1 8 2 2 0 2* and reached a forefinger for the Enter key.

But his finger hesitated just above the key. He stared at the small row of numbers on the screen. *You can just erase those numbers, push the exit key, and walk out of this office!* a small voice told him. *Just tell Grady you couldn't do it!*

Justin gave a quick shake of his head. It was too late now to back out! Setting his jaw with determination, he stabbed his finger at the Enter key.

For an instant he thought he must have hit the wrong key! Instead of filling up with the figures and diagrams Hacker had told him to expect, the screen went blank—just as it had at Grady's apartment. A warning beep clamored that something was wrong.

Justin stared with numb disbelief at the screen. Across the screen blazed the words: *IMPROPER PASSWORD. ACCESS DENIED!*

Justin stared in frozen panic at the message on the computer screen. What was he going to do now?

As the warning beep continued to announce his error, he forced himself to move. Frantically, he typed in one date after another—his own birthday, his father's, his parents' anniversary—his fingers fumbling as he calculated the numbers. But after each entry, the screen blinked once more: *IMPROPER PASSWORD. ACCESS DENIED.*

Dropping his head into his hands, Justin tried to think. But the warning beep distracted him. Miss Pettigrew must have heard it by now! She'd be in any moment to check out the signal. Or—maybe that beep had already notified the security system that someone was breaking into a classified file!

He tightened his fingers on his short-cropped curls until it hurt. What other happenings of importance had there been lately in the Parker household? The start of school? Or—

Justin sat up with sudden excitement. October 14, 1995—three days after his mother's birthday! That was the day the twins had helped Danny Nguyen bring about the arrest of the Dragon Tong, the Vietnamese gang that had terrorized the Nguyen family. Had that really been only a month ago?

A tap at the door brought Justin back to the present. Rapidly typing in the numbers *1 1 8 8 2 0 2,* he stabbed at the Enter key. The warning beep cut off immediately. Dropping his hands into his lap, he swiveled the chair around. When Miss Pettigrew thrust her head around the edge of the door, he was studying the spectacular view of the Seattle skyline through the plate-glass window behind his father's desk.

"Everything okay in here?"

Justin looked up, an innocent expression on his freckled face. Miss Pettigrew wrinkled her forehead. "I was sure I heard a computer beeping!"

"Everything's fine here!" Justin reassured her, but his hands were clenched in his lap. He put on a teasing grin. "Probably just your ears ringing. Overwork, you know! I'll tell Dad you need a day off!"

Miss Pettigrew ignored his attempt at humor. "Hmm! Must have been next door!" she muttered with a distracted frown.

She closed the door. The computer screen was now filled with unintelligible figures and diagrams. Consulting Hacker's instructions, he picked up the black pouch and took out the red disk. He was about to insert it when he hesitated. Maybe he'd better make sure he was doing this right before making that all-important copy for Grady!

Justin knew where Dad kept a box of new disks, already formatted. He'd borrowed one the last time he'd been in the office to copy off computer-generated pictures of the new Boeing 777. Digging into the bottom desk drawer, he pulled out a fresh disk and inserted it into the A-drive slot.

Justin moved the mouse to the figure which, according to Hacker's instructions, would allow him to copy the data onto the disk. Justin typed *Copy GP145 a: b:*. Moments later the screen announced *Files copied.* Justin was satisfied that the disk did indeed hold the data files Grady needed. Removing the disk, he inserted the red one and repeated the process. When the screen read *Files copied,* he took out the red disk and slid the blue one into the drive slot.

The blue disk was running smoothly. Justin leaned back in the office chair to wait. When the screen read *Program Finished,* he exited the GP145 project file. Taking out the blue disk, he shoved the instructions and disks into the black pouch.

He glanced at his watch. The whole process had taken less than ten minutes. He carefully positioned his father's swivel chair exactly as he had found it. Then he left the office.

He stopped at Miss Pettigrew's desk on the way out. "I can't wait any longer! But please don't tell him I was here. It would spoil the surprise!"

Miss Pettigrew glanced up from her computer terminal. She gave Justin a suspicious look.

"Oh, get out of here, Justin!" Miss Pettigrew tried to look annoyed. "You're holding up my work!"

Satisfied that his father's secretary would keep his secret, Justin took off at a run down the corridor. He bounded down the stairs two and three steps at a time. He'd succeeded after all! The precious copy of the invisibility shield plans was now safe in his hands.

"That surprise must have been a hit!" Charlie said, as Justin handed back the security pass.

Justin gave the guard a thumbs-up gesture. "Thanks!"

Justin headed for the bus stop. Should he go home or head back to school? Mom would be at home now. But if he showed up at school, he was likely to be faced with some awkward questions he was unable to answer!

He decided to take the bus home. He'd have to hang around outside until Jenny got home from school. But that was better than risking a run-in with an annoyed teacher.

Back at home, he could hear his mother singing in the kitchen. He spent the next several hours sitting under the huge, spreading oak tree across the street.

Justin pulled his jacket closer. A stiff November wind had risen, its dampness bringing with it a threat of rain. It had been a long time since breakfast, and he was getting colder and more ravenous by the minute. If this was how secret agents spent their days, then maybe he wouldn't take Grady up on his job offer after all!

Brushing the wet leaves from a protruding root, Justin leaned back against the massive trunk of the tree. At least it would soon be all over! Wouldn't Jenny's mouth drop open when Abdul's gang was finally arrested? Everyone would know then that Justin had saved them!

"So! You're back!"

Justin sprang to his feet so fast he banged his head on a low branch. "Ouch!" Rubbing the top of his head, he looked across at his sister. "Oh, hi, Jenny!"

Jenny was standing just beyond the shelter of the oak tree, her arms full of books and a backpack over each shoulder. She gave him a long, cool look. "So how did everything go this morning?"

"Just great!" Justin answered hastily. "Everything went fine!" He hurried over to lift his backpack from Jenny's shoulder. "How was school?"

"Okay. The teachers think you're sick." Jenny handed him a sheaf of papers. "I brought home all your assignments."

Shifting her remaining load to a more comfortable position, she started toward the house. "You'd better come on if you want Mom to think we were together."

"Uh, thanks a lot!" Swinging his backpack to his shoulder, Justin followed his sister. He had braced himself for Jenny's questions, and her lack of curiosity faintly alarmed him. But this wasn't the time to worry about it. He just hoped Grady hadn't called his house yet! He broke into a run.

"Any calls for me?" was his first anxious demand as he burst in the kitchen door.

Mom arched her eyebrows in surprise. "You don't usually get calls during school hours, Justin!"

Justin relaxed. Of course Grady would have realized that Justin couldn't come home until after school! His stomach growled as he smelled the fresh batch of chocolate-chip cookies. Dropping his backpack on the table, he reached for a handful.

He was reaching for a second when he heard a familiar engine turn in to the driveway. What was Dad doing back this early?

A car door slammed, then quick steps sounded in the gravel driveway. A moment later, Dad's tall figure appeared in the back doorway. Jenny gave him a cheerful wave. "Hi, Dad! How was work?"

But Dad didn't answer with his usual lighthearted greeting. Quietly shutting the back door, he stepped into the full sunlight of the kitchen window. Justin stiffened! He'd never seen that look on his father's face, and it frightened him!

Dad let his briefcase fall to the floor. Slumping into a kitchen chair, he dropped his head into his hands. Mom asked anxiously, "What is it, honey? Has something gone wrong with your project?"

Justin edged closer to his father. "Did someone steal it?"

Dad raised his head. His lean face looked grey. "Worse!" he said wearily. "It's been completely destroyed! Months of work—years of research—totally wiped out!"

Justin ignored the rest of his cookies. So it had finally happened—just like Grady had told him to expect! Abdul and his pals had stolen the GP145 and destroyed the files!

"But…but how could someone destroy an entire project?" Mom's dark eyes showed her concern and bewilderment. "All those guards…the security precautions!"

Dad reached over and took one of her hands. "It was a virus!"

A virus! Dad's words made perfect, horrible sense to Justin. A computer virus was a program designed—often by malicious pranksters—to be entered onto a computer hard drive. There it would destroy all or selected files in the computer's memory. If detected, a virus could be eliminated. But if a contaminated program was used without being checked, the virus could ruin the hard drive.

Dad wearily ran his fingers through his hair. "Someone has managed to design a virus that destroyed not just the computer file with our finished project plans, but every reference in the mainframe to this particular project. Months of work, years of research and data files, have been erased."

"But…that would take a genius!" Justin exclaimed.

"It would certainly take an expert!" Dad agreed. "What's more, an expert who knows an awful lot about the Boeing computer systems and the classified work going on there!"

He went on, "The first thing they did was to seal off the main computer banks and send everyone home. I have a feeling they're looking for an inside man—someone with access to the computer banks. You see, we had a phone block on the entire computer system. It would take someone inside the research facility—someone with very high clearance—to insert that virus program!"

Someone like Dad! Justin's stomach turned. No wonder the NSA had suspected his father!

A sudden thought lightened his worries. Whoever would be meeting Abdul that night to hand over the GP145, it wouldn't be his father! Justin still didn't understand how Abdul could have conned Dad into passing over classified information on computer disks. But Dad's present dismay made it clear that he knew nothing about the theft and destruction of the invisibility shield.

No, Abdul definitely had some other accomplice inside Boeing. Someone with the same computer skills as Dad. And when those stolen plans were handed over to Abdul tonight, Grady would be there to retrieve them!

Justin's spirits lifted at the thought of the sandy-haired NSA agent. So far Grady had been one step ahead of Abdul and his terrorist pals all the way! Abdul thought he'd destroyed the GP145 project. But thanks to Grady, the plans for the invisibility shield were sitting safe and sound under Justin's jacket. And when Grady stepped in tonight to arrest Abdul and his associate, Dad's innocence would be proven once and for all!

Justin shifted his feet restlessly. But where *was* Grady O'Brian? Was he keeping his own investigation under cover until he arrested Abdul that night? If only he'd call! The sooner those precious disks were out of his own hands, the better!

The feeling of someone's eyes on him made Justin glance up. His sister was watching him, an odd expression on her face. She looked quickly away. Moving to her father's side, she gave him a tight hug. "Please don't be so sad, Daddy! I'm sure they won't think *you* had anything to do with it!"

Dad hugged her back, but he shook his head. "That's where you're wrong, Jenny! I'm afraid everyone on that program who can handle a computer keyboard will be considered a possible suspect—including me!"

He managed a wry smile. "But that's the least of my worries! That project was of vital importance to our nation's security. Not only has it been destroyed, but it seems likely our computer expert stole a copy of the plans before he inserted that virus. In the wrong hands, those plans could mean grave danger for our country!"

Justin caught the worry in his eyes. If only he could reassure his father that everything would be all right! That the invisibility shield plans were safe, and in just a few hours, the thief who had stolen them would be in custody!

And why not? Dad wouldn't be seeing Abdul again before it was all over. There was nothing he could give away to the enemy now!

The front doorbell jangled. Mom hurried toward the living room. Justin turned to his father. "Dad—"

"Ron!" It was Mom. "There's someone here who wants to speak to you!"

Justin shut his mouth with a snap. He *would* get interrupted every time he tried to talk to his father! Dad was already on his feet. His long strides took him almost at a run into the living room.

Justin started after him, but now his sister was calling him back. Reluctantly, he slumped into a chair. "Yeah?" he growled. "What do you want?"

"I want to know what's going on!" Jenny gave him a cool look. "This project that got wrecked! That wouldn't happen to be the one you and Dad were talking about the other night, would it? Maybe this all has something to do with your little adventure this morning?"

But Justin's sharp ears had just caught the squeak of the front door swinging wide and the sound of footsteps entering the living room. "Shh!" He cut his sister off with a sharp wave of the hand. "Listen!"

Dad had left the kitchen door standing open just a few inches. Now both twins could hear a curt voice demanding, "Ron Parker? Dan Ramirez, National Security Agency!"

The *National Security Agency!* So Grady's investigation had at last come out into the open! Grady must have sent one of his agents to pick up the computer disks!

Justin jumped to his feet, but Jenny beat him to the kitchen door. Justin tried in vain to see over her shoulder. There was a low murmur of his parent's voices. Then he heard the curt voice again. "You have two choices, Mr. Parker! You can answer my questions right here, or you can come with us!"

Justin knit his eyebrows together. *This didn't sound right! What was Grady up to?*

Jenny pulled her head back, her brown eyes wide. "It's the police, or something! They're arresting Dad!"

But Justin was already pushing past her to peer around the kitchen door. Two men stood in the living room. Justin had no problem recognizing one of them. The man flashing a badge at his father was the driver of the brown van!

chapter eleven

Abdul's men here! And pretending to be NSA agents! Justin edged the door open a little farther. But what were they doing here?

Dad was already leading the two men across the living room. "Of course, I'll answer any questions you have!" he told the van driver with a friendly nod. "Have you found out yet how the files were stolen?"

"We have a pretty good idea, yes!" There was no answering friendliness in the other man's face. "May I sit down?"

Justin ducked back inside the kitchen. Somehow, he had to warn Dad! He didn't dare let the phony agents see him. But if he could call his father out of the room...

He bumped into Jenny, who was peering over his shoulder. Of course! He could send his sister into the living room.

"Jenny, could you—?"

But now it was Jenny who was waving Justin to silence. An angry exclamation brought them both crowding back to the door. Dad was on his feet.

"What do you mean, you traced unauthorized copies to my office? That's impossible! I wasn't even in the office this morning! And I assure you my secretary doesn't have access to my password!"

"Sit down, Mr. Parker!" the van driver ordered sternly. "We have proof!"

The twins exchanged a dismayed glance as Dad sank back down to the sofa. Justin's head was spinning.

"They think Dad's the one who wrecked that project!" Jenny hissed in his ear. "But that's crazy! There's no way anyone could get in…"

She stared at her brother, a suspicion dawning in her eyes. Justin felt a guilty flush creep up his neck. "Justin!" she whispered. "Where *were* you this morning?"

The shrill ring of the phone saved him. Justin motioned frantically for Jenny to answer it. He had to think! The traitor would have covered his tracks well. But any check of the computer log would be enough to turn up Justin's own intrusion into the mainframe computer. And Abdul's accomplice in Boeing must have tipped him off to that fact!

That's why those guys are here! Abdul knows someone else has a copy of the GP145! And he wants it!

"It's for you, Justin." Jenny waved the receiver. "Come on, Justin!" She repeated impatiently. "It's some man. He says it's important!"

Grady! He started for the hall. "I'll get it! Just a minute!"

Justin ran to his parents' bedroom and grabbed the phone beside the king-sized waterbed. "Grady, they're here!" he hissed.

"Who's there?" The sharp concern in Grady's voice was all Justin could have hoped for. "Those guys who were after you!" he explained. "Abdul's men! And they're pretending to be NSA agents!"

There was a silence on the other end of the line. Then Grady said, "I was afraid something like this might happen when they spotted you this morning! So, were you able to get the copy?"

"Sure! But now they know I've got it! At least, they think my dad does! They haven't seen me yet." Justin lowered his voice to a whisper. "Grady, I'm scared! Can't you come and arrest these guys?"

Grady's voice came calm and soothing over the line. "The problem is, I'm clear across Puget Sound—a two hour drive. I'll do what I can! But get yourself and those disks away from that house. *Now* before anyone sees you!"

Justin hesitated. He knew the vital importance of keeping the last remaining copy of the invisibility shield out of Abdul's hands. But how could he abandon his family to possible danger? If only he'd had a chance to warn Dad!

Grady sighed. "Look, Justin! There's a lot more at stake here than you or me—*or* your family. You've got to keep those disks out of Abdul's hands! Now, I'm sending a couple of my agents over there to pick up Abdul's men. Your family will be safe enough until they arrive. In the meantime, get out of there!"

Grady was right, as usual. And Justin had to admit that he too was more than anxious to get those disks out of the house and into the government agent's hands. "Okay, I'll leave right now. But where do I go? Your apartment?"

"Not the apartment! It's being watched!" There was a long pause on the line. Justin could make out a faint murmur of voices as though Grady was consulting with someone. He had to bite his lip to keep back his impatience. Then Grady was back on the line. "Can you make it down to the waterfront?"

"Yeah, I can take the bus, but—"

"Good! Meet me on the ferry wharf in one hour. If I'm not there, don't hang around waiting. Abdul may have someone watching! Just take the first ferry across Puget Sound to Bremerton. If I can't make it across, I'll meet you on this side."

With a click, Grady was gone. Justin hung up the receiver. Fortunately, so much had happened since he'd gotten home that he hadn't even had time to take off his jacket. The black pouch Hacker had given him was still tucked inside, and he had his bus pass and enough money for the ferry, if necessary.

He slipped back into the kitchen. Jenny wasn't there. Good! That would save an explanation.

Then he heard a cool voice say, "You have a son, I under-stand! About thirteen or fourteen years old, with red hair?"

Justin's blood ran cold! The driver of the van was asking for him! Scrambling for the back door, he paused only long enough to pull it shut silently behind him.

Justin ran until he reached the end of the block. Then he stretched his legs in a sprint for the bus stop. A bus was pulling up when he got there. Threading his way to the back, Justin kept an anxious watch out the rear window. But he saw no sign of the brown van, and, after ten minutes, he got off and boarded another bus that would take him straight to the Seattle waterfront. Dropping into an empty seat, he leaned back and took a deep breath. The bus wouldn't reach the waterfront for another forty minutes. Now at last he could relax!

But Justin's thoughts were far from pleasant as he stared out across six lanes of freeway traffic. Things had gotten so complicated!

I'm glad I made those copies. he told himself stoutly. *If I hadn't, Dad's project would be gone for good!*

But he couldn't stop the fears that churned in his mind. Had Grady told anyone that he'd had Justin break into the Boeing computer? That program he'd inserted for Hacker was supposed to trace the real traitor. But that could take time!

In the meantime, if Abdul and his men had so quickly assumed that Dad had made that unauthorized copy of the GP145 files, then the investigative team must have come to the same conclusion. Instead of clearing his father's name, he'd gotten him into even more trouble!

Justin pressed the back of his hands against his eyes. Grady knew that Dad hadn't made that unauthorized copy. But until Grady informed his superiors that *he* was the one responsible, no one would believe that Dad was innocent.

Justin's head ached badly by the time he got off the bus not far from the ferry docks. The sky was overcast, and a chill sea breeze bit through his clothes. He pulled his jacket tight, his nostrils flaring at the sharp tang of salt. But the fresh air blew away his headache, and suddenly the answer to his dilemma was clear!

With a lighter heart, Justin trotted along the waterfront. He stopped at Ye Olde Curiosity Shop long enough to buy an envelope and a postage stamp. Pulling out the black pouch, he checked the disks inside. They sure didn't look worth all the fuss being made over them!

"Would you have a scrap of paper and a pen I could borrow? he asked the clerk. "I need to write my parents!"

"Sure!" The clerk set a paper and pen on the counter. Justin scribbled a quick letter to his parents. He hadn't dared risk a note earlier, not with those phony NSA agents in the house. But if something should go wrong, he wanted them to know where he was going—and why!

"Great! Thanks a million!" Justin broke into a run, pausing only long enough to thrust the envelope through the slot of the nearest mailbox.

He checked his watch as he skidded to a stop in front of the ferry terminal. It was five o'clock, exactly an hour since Grady's call.

Shielding his eyes against the setting sun, Justin looked around. He saw no sign of the government agent, but a ferry was approaching the pier, its blunt prow churning the choppy waves into a white froth. Maybe Grady was on that boat!

Justin made his way into the terminal. It was even more crowded than the wharf as lines of commuters jostled to buy tickets for the next ferry. He was standing on tiptoe to scan the crowd when he stopped short.

Only a few feet away, two Arab men argued in low, passionate voices.

One of the Arabs turned in Justin's direction. His eyes widened and he muttered a quick phrase to his companion. Justin ducked into the crowd as the other Arab turned to stare in his direction. His thoughts flew to the two Middle Eastern tourists he'd seen on his last visit to the ferry wharf. *Could these be the same guys? If so, they must be Abdul's men! Grady had said someone might be watching!*

But the two men made no move to follow him. A blare of sound overhead announced that the incoming ferry was disembarking. Justin trotted across the terminal to watch the foot passengers crowd their way through the big double doors. When the last passenger had pushed past him without a sign of Grady, he hurried to buy a ticket. There was nothing more to do but obey Grady's instructions and take the ferry back across Puget Sound to Bremerton.

Justin leaned his elbows on the metal rail of the ship. The sun had disappeared behind the far shoreline, and the water looked grey and cold. The waves were choppy and crested with foam, rougher than he'd ever seen them.

Overhead, a seagull gave his wild, lonely cry. Sudden tears pricked at Justin's eyes. Never had he felt so alone! Jenny, at least, had always been at his side on every other adventure. As the twilight darkened to night, he stared out across the water with unseeing eyes. *What if Grady wasn't on the other side either? What then?*

Quick footsteps echoed across the metal deck. "Justin?"

Justin spun around. "Grady! Wh…where were you? I thought I'd missed you!"

The government agent clapped Justin on the shoulder. "I saw you looking for me, but I decided to wait for you to board the ferry." He held out his hand. "You got the disks?"

Justin nodded, sliding one hand into the front of his jacket. The sight of the government agent had lifted his worries. He'd soon be rid of the disks and the whole mess. But there was still one thing he had to do!

Pulling out the black pouch, he unzipped it to show Grady a glimpse of red and blue. The stocky agent stared down at the pouch, an odd, unreadable expression on his face. He whistled softly. "So you've really done it! I honestly didn't think you could! Good job, Justin!"

He reached for the pouch, but Justin snatched it away. Zipping it back up, he stuffed it inside his jacket. "I'm sorry, Grady! I can't let you have them. Not yet, anyway!"

Grady couldn't hide his exasperation. "Just give me the pouch!"

Justin backed along the ferry rail just out of reach. "I can't!"

Taking a deep breath, he launched into the speech he'd been rehearsing. "You asked me to help you catch those terrorists! Well, I've done everything you've asked! Not just to help my father, but…well, because of all that stuff about the security of the United States! Now I want you to do something for me! And…and I can't give you the disks until you do it!"

"Why you little—" Grady took a purposeful step forward, his square features hardening with anger. Justin backed farther away along the rail. For one long moment, the man and the boy locked eyes. Justin's heart pounded, but he met the steel-grey gaze without flinching.

It was Grady who dropped his gaze first. Some of the anger left his face. "Maybe you do deserve something for your help!" Grady said with a shrug. "It's not the first time we've had to pay off an informant! So what do you want? A new bike? Cash?"

"Of course not!" Justin's back was stiff with outrage. "I don't want anything for me! I want you to tell those guys who are investigating that you're the one who made me copy those files. And I want you to tell the National Security Agency that my dad's innocent!"

"And risk tipping off our traitor at Boeing?" Grady answered sharply. "He still has to turn those plans over to Abdul! I've already told you I'd take care of your father, but can't this wait a few hours?"

"Then I'll hold onto the disks until you do!" Justin's freckled face was stubborn. "I mean, you said you just needed the plans so you could arrest Abdul! Well, I've got 'em, so go ahead and arrest him!"

Justin paused to take a breath. To his relief, Grady no longer looked angry. He stumbled on. "You told me even your bosses think my dad's guilty! I can't give you the disks until I know Dad's out of trouble!"

"Then we'll have to take them!"

Justin swung around with a gasp. He groaned inwardly when he caught sight of Hacker leaning against the ship rail.

Hacker sauntered toward Justin, an ugly smile playing around his mouth. Justin ducked behind Grady.

"Stay away from me!" he panted. "Or I'll never give you the disks!"

"You are having some trouble?"

The question in strongly accented English brought Justin's head around with a jerk. It was the same two Arabs he had seen arguing in the ferry terminal.

Forgetting Hacker and the black pouch, Justin clutched at Grady's arm. "Grady, those men! I saw them on the wharf! They must have followed me here!"

The two olive skinned gentlemen walked toward them. One of the men carried a large briefcase. Justin drew in a sharp breath as the other man's coat flapped open, exposing a shoulder holster underneath. "Grady, they've got guns! They must be Abdul's men!"

But Grady's square features showed only irritation as he turned to face the two newcomers. "What are you doing here?" he snapped. "I told you I'd meet you tonight!"

"We have a right to protect our investment," one man said. His English was slow but clear.

"You know these guys?" Justin relaxed his grip on Grady's sleeve. "Then they were with *you* that day in the Curiosity Shop! I was sure they worked for Abdul!"

"Abdul?" The second Arab stepped forward, his black eyes hard with suspicion. "Who is this Abdul, Grady O'Brian? Have you sold this—what do you call it—'invisibility shield' to a competitor?"

"Sell?" Justin looked up at Grady, a slow, cold fear rising in his stomach. "What's he talking about?"

Grady ignored the question. Turning, he jerked his head toward Justin. "The boy's got the plans. Do you have the money?"

Justin stared appalled. His gaze swept from the two Arabs to the government agent.

"Grady, what are you saying?" he whispered. "That *you* stole the invisibility shield? That...that there never *was* a traitor in Boeing?"

"Just you, Justin!" Grady answered cheerfully. "And you've been kind enough to deliver the plans right into our hands!"

chapter twelve

Justin pressed backward, his mind spinning dizzily. This had to be a nightmare!

"Grady!" he pleaded, still in a whisper. "You're joking!"

"Oh, it's no joke! These two men are representatives of a Middle Eastern political faction. They've commissioned me to obtain the GP145." Grady was smiling—that same heartwarming grin that had won Justin over from the start. But this time Justin didn't respond.

"You mean, they're terrorists!" he said bitterly, stuffing his hands in his pockets to warm them.

His mind was still reeling. How could he be a traitor?

He shook his head with bewilderment. "I don't get it! You showed me your I.D.! That badge was from the National Security Agency, just like you said! And that stuff about the invisibility shield—about my dad's work! It was all true! If you're not a real agent, how could you know all that?"

"Oh, I was a government agent, all right." Grady said cheerfully. "That is, until a few years back. The credentials were from my Agency days. As for the invisibility shield, an old military contact let me in on that. When I found a buyer, I started working on a plan to get the GP145 file."

"Then you really were going to kidnap my dad!" Justin said. The conversation he'd overheard a few days earlier now made sense. "That's why you were following us!"

"That was our first plan." Grady threw a disgusted look at

Hacker. "Thanks to this idiot's faulty information! *You* messed up that attempt! Not that I'm complaining. Your little interference was the best piece of luck we've had! Anyway, once we found out your father was no scientist, Hacker here tried to break into the mainframe computer. When that didn't work—well, you know the rest."

Justin *did* know the rest! He felt sick as he realized how completely the renegade agent had tricked him. And if the two Arabs hadn't walked in, he'd have handed over those disks without ever guessing what Grady really was!

The former agent held out his hand again. "Look, Justin, you've been a great help, and I really don't want to hurt you. Just give me those disks, and you can walk right on out of here."

The smile in his grey eyes was so friendly that for one instant Justin found himself reaching into his jacket for the black pouch. Then a sudden, horrible picture—a picture of invisible missiles and fighter planes launched against an unsuspecting United States—broke the spell of that compelling voice. How could he have believed for a moment that these men would let him walk out of there to warn the police?

He glanced around desperately. There had to be someone on this crowded ferry who could help him! But the other passengers were all up on the observation decks, and the four men who surrounded him blocked any dash for freedom.

Folding his arms across his jacket, he glared his defiance at Grady. "I'll never give you these disks! Touch me and I'll scream!"

But Grady only laughed. "Go ahead and scream. If someone comes, they're not going to be too happy about being dragged down here by some disobedient kid who's run off with his dad's office documents. And with three witnesses, I don't think anyone's going to believe you're not really my son!"

Justin hesitated. Would any passerby believe his accusations of spies and international plots against the word of all these adults? Even to him, the story sounded incredible.

"So you see, Justin," Grady was still smiling, "You really *will* have to hand over those disks. The Arab Front for World Liberation isn't known for its patience!"

He gave a nod, and Hacker and the two others closed in on Justin. But before they could grab him, Justin snatched the black pouch from inside his jacket. Holding the pouch over the rail, he said hoarsely, "Get back! I'll drop it if you don't!"

With a sharp hand gesture, Grady ordered the three men back. They obeyed, scowling and muttering angrily to each other. But Hacker only sneered, "He's bluffing! That's the last copy of his dad's project. He wouldn't destroy it!"

"I'm not bluffing!" Justin's voice rose shrill and loud despite his efforts to seem calm. "I'd rather no one had the invisibility shield than you guys!"

"No, he's not bluffing." Grady said shortly, watching Justin with narrowed eyes. He motioned Hacker back.

"This is ridiculous!" Hacker snarled, obeying with obvious reluctance. His thin hands were clenching and unclenching at his sides.

But Grady was looking more amused than angry. "Okay, Justin, I guess we're at a stalemate. You're not going to give us those disks, and we're not about to walk away and leave you with them."

He leaned back against a nearby car. "I think you'll get tired of holding that pouch out there before we get tired of waiting!"

With dismay, Justin realized that Grady was right. Already, his arm was aching from holding the pouch out over the boiling froth of the ferry wake. He threw a frantic glance over his shoulder. It was night now, but directly ahead he could make out Deer Island looming almost invisibly against the blackness of the overcast sky. A few distant lights clearly marked the ranger station and ferry dock.

Justin glanced again at the growing bulk of the island. The ferry soon would be docking to pick up the last of the day's sightseers, and he knew Grady's threat of claiming him as his son was not idle. If he didn't make a move in the next few minutes, any chance of keeping the disks out of the terrorists' hands would be lost! Dropping his eyes to the churning foam that bubbled up ghostly-white around the bow of the ferry, he had a sudden desperate idea. If he could just keep Grady talking!

"Uh…Grady? There's still one thing I don't get. If you're working for these guys, then who's Abdul? Were you trying to sell him the invisibility shield, too?"

"Abdul! Again, this Abdul!" The Arab with the briefcase took a threatening step toward Grady, his eyes flashing. "Who is this man? You promised to deal with no other buyer!"

"I haven't the slightest idea who this Abdul is!" Grady looked annoyed as the terrorist muttered an angry phrase in Arabic to his partner. "Just some foreigner I saw talking to Ron Parker. He's probably some Third World diplomat begging for technical assistance from Boeing!"

"What! You mean, Abdul isn't a spy at all?" Justin almost dropped the pouch. "But…you knew all about him. You told me his name."

"*You* told me his name!" Grady said softly as he broke off. "You were so sure that Arab looked like a terrorist. A piece of luck that made it a lot easier to get your help!"

Red crept up Justin's neck, but he went on doggedly. "Then those guys at my house—the brown van that was following us— they're not Abdul's men? They really are from the National Security Agency?"

Grady grinned. "My old Agency buddies. Something must have tipped them off that I was going after the invisibility shield. That's one more thing I owe you, Justin! They'd have had me this morning at the apartment if you hadn't tipped me off."

"I wish I'd let them catch you." Justin muttered. A quick glance told him that the dark outline of Deer Island was now much closer, and he added hurriedly, "But—the virus! If there wasn't any real spy in Boeing, then who destroyed those files? My dad said it took a real computer whiz to put that virus together."

A mocking laugh exploded from the shadows to his left.

Justin twisted to stare at Hacker, who was lounging against the rail, a contemptuous sneer on his thin lips. "You! *You* made that virus! But how could you get it into the computers? You'd have had to be inside the research facility."

Then a horrible realization squeezed at his stomach. "Oh, no!" he whispered. "*I* did it, didn't I? That blue disk. If there wasn't any traitor, then that program had to be—"

Justin could no longer contain his anger. "You used *me* to ruin my dad's whole project!" he exploded.

Hacker's sneer slipped for an instant under Justin's outraged glare. Turning his back, he demanded angrily, "Are we going to put up with this all night, Grady? Just grab the kid and get those disks!"

But Grady cut him off with a sharp motion of his hand. Still grumbling, Hacker subsided and Justin took a deep breath. He thought he'd felt the ferry begin to slow. If only the others hadn't noticed!

Thrusting his arm further over the rail, he turned back to Grady. "So why'd you do it, Grady? How could you betray your country after all that talk about national security?"

Grady gave a short, humorless laugh. "The only security I care about now is my own. Oh, yes, I'm in it for the money. That briefcase over there has a few million dollars in it that's going to keep me comfortable for the rest of my life!"

He straightened up from the side of the car. "Come on, Justin. Am I really such a bad guy? I haven't let these guys hurt you, have I? And I wouldn't worry so much about national security. By the time the Arab Front for World Liberation ever figures out how to use the invisibility shield, I'm sure your father and his friends will have found a way to neutralize it. Look, I'll even share with you—say, fifty-thousand dollars?"

A flicker of movement from the corner of his eye brought his head up with a jerk. He caught his breath in alarm. While Grady had held his attention, Hacker and the Arabs had been circling around to close in on him. The one-time government agent had fooled him again!

Making a desperate lunge for the pillar that supported the deck above, Justin hauled himself onto the rail. The metal deck rail was slick with salt spray, but he managed to pull himself to a standing position. His stomach heaved in rhythm with the ferry as he looked out across the rolling darkness of the Sound.

He swayed. The waves rushed up at him. Through a roaring in his ears, he heard Grady shout, "Get down from there, you fool! Someone get that kid down before he falls!"

Hands grabbed at his ankles. Justin kicked out with all his strength. Drawing in a deep breath, he took one last glance at the white froth below. Then, as hands snatched at him again, he jumped!

chapter thirteen

The water closed over Justin's head, the shock of its winter chill driving the breath from his lungs. The frothing bubbles tore at him, tumbling him over and over as though he were caught in a giant's washing machine. He kicked upward, snorting as the saltwater stung his nostrils. But he hadn't reckoned with the sheer force of the water churned by the passing ferry.

It's pulling me under the boat! Justin struck out frantically, suddenly panic-stricken as he fought the pressure that pushed him deep below the surface of the water. His lungs burned with his need for air. Then, just as he knew he would have to inhale— even if it meant his lungs filling with sea water—a last, desperate kick carried him beyond the turbulence of the ferry wake.

Breaking the surface of the water, he gasped in a long, shuddering breath. The ferry was still sliding past him only a few yards to his right. Justin could make out several dark forms silhouetted against the deck lights. They were running along the edge of the car deck toward the rear of the ferry.

"I have seen him!" The guttural foreign accent rang out over the water. The running figures crowded to the back rail. Then something smacked the water only inches from Justin's head. As the ferry's circle of light moved away, another smack sprayed his face with saltwater.

They're shooting at me! They're using silencers! Reacting at last, Justin dove deep beneath the surface. He stayed under until his lungs were bursting. When he broke the surface again, the ferry was gone. Even the glow of its lights had disappeared beyond the tossing waves.

Just in front of him a wave crested, its tip foaming ghostly-white. Curling over, it slapped him full in the face. Justin went under again, sputtering and snorting. He struggled back to the surface, gagging on the seawater that filled his throat. Shaking his head to clear his eyes, he looked around for the black bulk of Deer Island.

But it wasn't there! A bitter wind, reaching Puget Sound from a winter squall far out to sea, lashed the salt water to a frenzy. The heavy swells that had looked so rough from the ferry deck now rose high above Justin's bobbing head!

A slow drizzle pattered against his upturned face. No hint of moon or starlight filtered through the rain-swollen clouds. He was swimming now in a rolling, heaving darkness so black he could barely make out the hand he waved in front of his eyes.

Justin knew that Deer Island lay only a few hundred yards away. But caught in the trough between two long rollers, all he could see was the faint glimmer of the cresting waves. *Where was the island?*

He tried to still his chattering teeth, to think clearly. His plan had seemed so easy from the ferry deck. He would jump into the water when the ferry neared Deer Island. He was a good swimmer and could easily swim a few hundred yards. Once on shore, he could make his way to the ranger station. There it would just be a matter of calling his parents and the police.

But now, unable to see the black outline of the island above the frenzied waves, he didn't even know which way to swim. And already the bitter chill of the seawater bit through his clothes. He couldn't last long in these icy waters!

Then suddenly, a surging wave caught him from underneath, tossing him high. He gasped as he glimpsed the warm glow of the Seattle skyline far off to his right, the Space Needle rising against the night sky. To his left was the welcome twinkle of the ranger station, the lighted silhouette of the ferry bobbing at its nearby docks.

Turning his back on the distant outline of the city, Justin began swimming toward those lights. Doggedly, he climbed to the top of each heavy swell, then dropped again into a darkness that left him once more disoriented. Only when a larger-than-usual roller lifted him high was he able to make out the silhouette of Deer Island. Then he corrected his course and swam on.

He'd been kicking and struggling for what seemed hours when he realized that the twinkling safety of the ranger station never seemed to draw any closer. In fact, each fresh glimpse of those distant lights seemed to have drifted farther off to his right. He'd been caught in an ocean current! Justin kicked with a new desperate strength. He had to reach the shore before that current swept him past the island!

He'd covered more than half the distance when he realized he might not make it! What would have been an easy swim on a warm summer day was a different matter with winter temperatures only a few degrees above freezing. His arms and legs moved only mechanically now. Some far-off corner of his mind wondered dully if the black pouch was still inside his jacket. But his hands were too frozen to feel for it. His whole body was numb with cold and exhaustion. Each time a wave crashed over his head, it took longer to struggle back to the surface.

Then slowly, the water seemed to warm. The burning chill left his limbs. In fact, he no longer felt much of anything except an overwhelming desire to sleep! He stopped swimming. If he could just float here a few minutes! Maybe close his eyes for a short rest!

Hypothermia! A slow realization of danger crept into his sluggish brain. The sleepiness and false sense of warmth were the signals of a dangerously low body temperature! He *had* to get out of these icy waters—and fast!

Justin tread water long enough to kick off his shoes. This was more difficult than he'd expected since he could no longer feel his feet. But the relief of that weight gave him strength to begin swimming again.

A swell rose beneath him, carrying him up, up—farther than he had yet been. The lights of the ranger station were still far to his right, but his numbed mind slowly registered the crash of waves against a rocky shore somewhere ahead. *You're almost there! You've got to keep going!*

But his frozen limbs no longer obeyed him! Helplessly, he slid down the other side of the wave. With sleepy fascination, he stared up at the slope of the wave. It was bigger than he'd thought, swollen perhaps by the rising tide and the storm out at sea. And it seemed to be growing, reaching above him in a black, menacing peak!

As Justin watched, the huge mass of salt water curved slowly inward, the foam on its tip reaching a long, ghostly hand down toward him. Only then did some instinct of self-preservation shock his brain awake. *Oh, no! It's breaking! And I'm underneath!*

But Justin couldn't force himself to move! Like a slow-motion replay, the breaking wave curled in on itself. For one endless moment, it seemed to hang there, the foam-crested tip far above his head.

Then gravity won its battle, and thousands of pounds of sea-water crashed down in a boiling, frothing lather. This time, Justin no longer had the strength even to lift his head. As the weight of the water carried him below the surface, something long and slimy reached up to wrap itself around his ankles.

With dull surprise he realized, *I'm drowning!*

chapter fourteen

Justin floated face down. Wave after wave tugged at his body, bumping him slowly forward. Something sharp scratched his cheek. The sudden pain brought him to full consciousness again. It was a long moment before he realized that it was sand and rock that scraped at his body. Something solid lay under his frozen hands.

Somehow Justin struggled to his feet. Pulling away the strand of seaweed that had wrapped itself around his ankles, he staggered through the breakers toward the shore.

There was no real beach, just a steep, rock-strewn bank slanting up to the hiking trail that ran around the island. Justin had been swept far to his left by the current, and the lights of the ranger station were now hidden around the curve of the island. Pushing through the tangle of brush that edged the shore, he sprawled onto the smooth surface of the path.

But he knew he couldn't lie there for long. The brush and trees around him cut off the chill sea wind, but it was still not much warmer here than in the water. As feeling crept back into his arms and legs, he began to shiver. He had to get to the warmth and shelter of the ranger station!

Stumbling to his feet, Justin opened his jacket a few inches and felt inside. To his relief, the pouch was still there. Tucking his numbed hands into his armpits, he started down the path in a shambling trot.

A foghorn blared as the path opened onto the park land that

sloped to the ranger station. The ferry's twinkling outline was just disappearing around the curve of the island as it headed for the far shore of Puget Sound.

The last ferry of the day! he thought forlornly, wiping the drizzle from his face with a wet sleeve. *How will I get home?*

But as he started down the grassy slope, he decided it was just as well the ferry had gone on without him. *At least I won't have to worry about running into Grady and his goons!*

At the bottom of the slope, he trotted along the wooden boardwalk that edged the water. The scattered buildings of the ranger station were dark except for the small, wood-framed house where the park ranger lived. The welcoming glow of those windows pulled Justin like a magnet. In just a few moments, he'd be warm and safe. He'd call Dad, and this whole nightmare would be at an end!

The porch was lit by one small bulb. Running eagerly up the front steps, Justin raised a fist to hammer on the door.

Grady's cold, angry voice stopped him short. "I told you not to shoot the kid! If we don't get those plans, it's going to cost your necks!"

Justin stood paralyzed with shock, one hand still raised. Then the sound of quick footsteps sent him diving for cover. He ducked behind a rain barrel set under the nearest window just as the front door creaked open. Grady's frowning face peered out into the darkness, then the door slammed shut.

"I thought I heard someone," he heard Grady say. "Maybe it's the boy!"

"He never came up after those shots!" Hacker's voice snapped. "He probably drowned. Ten million dollars down the drain!"

Raising his head cautiously, Justin peered over the edge of the windowsill. He looked into the park ranger's cozy home. A fire crackled merrily in the stone fireplace. Justin eyed the dancing flames with longing. He was so cold!

But the rest of the scene wasn't as cozy. There were five men in the room. Hacker lounged in an armchair near the fire, a cigarette in his thin fingers. Near the door stood the two Arabs, their guns hanging loosely from their hands. One still carried the briefcase chained to his wrist.

The fifth man was the young park ranger Justin had seen with his parents the first day he'd met Grady. The ranger sat slumped over, blood trickling from a cut over one eye. Grady was winding a length of rope around his wrists and ankles.

I should have known! Justin told himself savagely. Grady and his men must have guessed that he'd head straight for the island.

But now they too were stranded on the island. Would they really stay until the first ferry the next day?

Justin soon found out. Giving a last tug to the knots that bound the young park ranger, the renegade secret agent pulled what looked like a small transistor radio from a pocket and tossed it to one of the terrorists. "Let your friends know we'll be a bit late! We've got to search the island for the kid!"

"Aw, come on! It's raining out there!" Hacker protested, lighting another cigarette from the stub of the last one. "Besides, those disks will be worthless after a dunking in seawater! Just call in the yacht and get us out of here."

"I'm not stupid!" Grady retorted coldly. "That pouch I gave the kid was waterproof. If he's made it to the island, then those plans are still good!"

They have a yacht out there! Justin realized as the man pulled an antenna to full length and spoke tersely in Arabic. *That's how they're going to get those plans out of the country!*

Ducking away from the window, Justin ran along the side of the house. He was shaking, as much from fear as from cold.

Silently, he slipped around the back. Somehow, he had to keep those disks away from the terrorists. But first he had to get warm! If only he could find an old tarp or rug.

He trotted through the night toward what looked like a tool shed when he tripped. Biting back a startled yelp, he ran cautious hands over what had blocked his way. His heart raced with sudden excitement as he recognized the distinct feel of wool beneath his hands. He had stumbled into an old blanket hanging from a clothesline!

Yanking down the blanket, he wrapped it around his shoulders. It was damp and smelled strongly of wood smoke and fish. But Justin didn't care. Now all he needed was a place to hide. And he knew just where to go!

He climbed back up the slope toward the shelter of the woods just in time. A door crashed open behind him. He had reached the entrance to the hiking path when he heard Grady shout, "That blanket's gone! He's here all right! Split up and search both sides of the island."

Justin knew he had to leave the trail. But first he had to find what he was looking for.

There! He'd almost missed it in the dark. The path dipped right down to the shore here, forming a flat, rocky beach where he and Jenny had often dug for shells and ocean-polished rocks when they were small. That funny boulder that always made Jenny think of a squat, fat Santa Claus was still there, a black outline against the faint glimmer of the breakers.

Turning away from the beach, Justin ducked into the bushes on the far side of the path. In a straight line from that squat boulder was their secret hideout—a cave carved into the tangled roots of two ancient trees.

They'll never find me there! If only I can find it! Suddenly a beam of light dazzled his eyes. Instinctively, Justin dropped to a crouch. Above his head, the powerful flashlight played back and forth through the woods. A murmur of voices reached his ears from the path that was still only a short distance away.

At last, the light disappeared, and Justin rose to his feet. He bit his lip as he stepped on a sharp twig. Now that his feet were throbbing back to life, he could feel every scrape and bruise.

Ignoring the pain, he pushed farther into the brush. Branches left scratches of red across one cheek, but he didn't dare slow his pace. It wouldn't take long for Grady and his men to search the footpath and shore. He had to find that hiding place soon!

He was beginning to despair when he suddenly stumbled into the open. Stifling a gasp of thankfulness, he peered into the darkness. Yes, this had to be the spot. The hideout should to be straight ahead!

But he had taken only a few steps across the clearing when he froze. He listened without breathing. Yes, there it was! The deep whoosh of an exhaled breath! Then he heard a faint rustle in the grass. Someone—or something—was in the dark glade with him!

The rustle moved closer. The blood pounded in Justin's ears, and he had to dig his fingernails into the palms of his hands to keep from panicking. *Was one of Grady's men standing nearby in the darkness, waiting for him? Or…could it be some wild animal, maybe a bear or a mountain lion?*

Then something cool and moist nuzzled softly at his hand. Justin felt a smooth, warm head with two small buds of horn under his fingers. With another soft whoosh, a yearling deer snuffled at his pockets for the food it had come to expect from visitors to the island.

Pushing the deer away, Justin hurried across the clearing until he reached the bushes on the other side. Dropping to his hands and knees, he groped his way until his fingers met a gnarled tangle of protruding tree roots. He'd found the hideout!

But was the den still empty? What if it was the home to some animal—a fox or a wolverine? Justin sat back on his heels, but a shout jerked his head up in alarm. He could see a distant gleam of light probing the woods to his left. He would just have to take his chances!

Dropping to his belly, he wormed his way under the brush, then shifted and slid his legs into the hollow.

From inside, Justin tore off a small branch and swept any tracks he'd left outside the thicket. Only then did he slide all the way into the hideout. It was empty. He'd been afraid that the hole would be too small for a husky thirteen-year-old. But once he squeezed through the narrow opening, he found that he could even sit up, his head pressed against the root system that roofed the den.

Now he began to shiver again. He pulled the blanket tight, tucking the ends under his scratched and bruised feet. His stomach cramped with hunger, reminding him that he hadn't eaten since that handful of cookies he'd snatched from the kitchen. He settled back against the wall of the den.

Justin was miserable. He'd escaped Grady and his men for the moment. But who was he kidding? They had only to wait till daybreak to trace his tracks to this clearing. And unlike his past adventures, he had no hope this time that someone would show up to rescue him. No one—not even Jenny—had the slightest idea where he was!

"Justin! Hey, kid!" The shouts echoed through the woods outside the den. Justin raised his head warily as Grady and his men tried to coax him into the open.

"Look, kid! We know you're out there!" Justin stiffened. It was Hacker! A faint glow from the entrance lit the blackness of the den. Hacker was right outside!

The glow of a flashlight beam grew brighter. Someone was approaching his hiding place!

Now, Grady's voice coaxed him. "Look, Justin, you're cold and hungry. You know you can't last out here till morning. Why don't you come on in where it's warm?"

Justin gritted his teeth, stuffing his fists into his ears to shut out that friendly, sympathetic sound. *Did Grady really think he'd fall for his lies again?*

Justin dropped his hands as the men moved away. He sifted back through the events of the last weeks. Now that he knew what Grady was, he could see how the agent had tricked him into helping him steal the GP145.

One consoling thought lightened his misery. At least Grady's threats of arresting his father had also been a lie! There never had been a traitor on the Boeing research team!

But wait! There was a traitor! Justin sat up, hitting his head on the roof overhead so hard it brought tears to his eyes. *He* was the Boeing traitor, just as Grady had said! By taking the GP145, he'd endangered the safety of his entire country.

And if Dad *had* been in no danger of arrest, that was no longer true. Not after what Justin had done that morning. Not now that the NSA was convinced Dad had stolen the invisibility shield plans and destroyed years of vital research!

Choking back a sob, Justin dropped his head to his knees. *God, why did You let this happen? It's all Your fault! You knew Grady was lying! Why didn't You help me?*

Huddled with his head bowed, Justin realized this was the first time since this nightmare had begun that he had prayed. And as the tears squeezed their way from under his closed eyelids, it was as though a quiet, gentle voice answered, *You never asked Me.*

No, he'd never asked God's help in this mess! In spite of the trouble he had thought his father was in, the renegade government agent had made him feel important. Justin burned with shame.

And instead of asking God for help, he'd lied! To his parents, to his sister, to his teachers! Then he'd defended his actions by saying that he had no choice!

If I hadn't lied, Dad would have told me Abdul was no spy. He'd have known about Grady in time to keep him from stealing the invisibility shield.

Clenching his fists, Justin prayed silently, *Oh, God, I'm so sorry! I thought I had to lie to help my dad! But I was wrong! Please forgive me and…well, I know I don't deserve it. But won't You please help my dad and keep those men from getting his project?*

Nothing had changed inside the cramped den. He was just as hungry, and this hole in the ground was just as damp and crowded. But Justin was suddenly comforted. He wasn't really alone. God was with him, and He had forgiven him.

He felt almost warm now. The exhaustion and emotion of the last hours were catching up with him. His eyes drooped shut. He was almost asleep.

"Justin! Justin, where are you!" The whisper was low and not very far away.

"Come on, Justin, where are you?"

Justin jerked awake as the whispered call was repeated. His eyes strained against the blackness of the den. If it was one of Grady's men out there, he didn't carry a flashlight. But why bother whispering?

"Justin, I know you're there! Come on! Answer me!" The whisper drifted closer. Justin tensed. Someone was searching the brush just outside his hiding place!

Justin didn't dare even breathe. *If he doesn't see anything, maybe he'll go away!*

But already he'd caught the scraping, dragging sound of someone creeping under the brush! Then he heard the patter of falling dirt. A small pebble rolled down the entrance to stop at Justin's feet. His hiding place had been discovered!

They won't get me that easily! Shifting to a crouch, Justin groped around in the dark. His hand slid across a stone. A soft, hurried breathing told him that his unseen visitor was inching headfirst into the hideout. His heart was racing, but he lifted the rock above his head. *When the guy gets close enough, I'll smash his head in!*

His muscles tensed, the rock ready. Then a soft voice hissed, "Justin? It's me, Jenny. Are you in here?"

Justin's mouth dropped open in the darkness. The stone fell from his fingers. He whispered in amazement, "Jenny! How did you get here?"

"I followed you." Sliding forward on her stomach, Jenny pulled herself the rest of the way into the den. The fit was tight, but there was just enough room for her to sit with her legs pulled up.

Reaching into the darkness, Justin touched a tangle of curls, then brushed his fingers across her face. "Jenny, you're crying! Are you okay?"

"I'm *not* crying!" Jenny whispered crossly. But she sniffed and then muttered, "I thought you'd drowned!"

"I almost did." Sliding an arm around her shoulders, Justin gave her a brotherly squeeze. Then he returned with bewilderment to his first question. "I don't get it. How did you know where I was?"

"I was on the other line when you were talking to...what did you call him? Oh, yeah, Grady! When he told you to meet him at the ferry wharf with the plans for Dad's invisibility thing, I left and took a bus straight there."

Justin's mouth was still open as she went on. "You never even noticed me following you at the terminal! When that Grady didn't come, I knew you'd have to take the ferry so I bought a ticket and boarded ahead of you. I was hiding under one of the cars when Grady and those other guys showed up. I was going to get the captain when you jumped over the rail. Then I heard one of the men say he'd shot you!"

Jenny's whispered explanation wobbled. She steadied her voice. "I was afraid you'd drowned. But I knew you'd head for the island if you were still alive, so I followed Grady and hid under the wharf until the ferry left. Then I heard them shouting that you had to be here. With all those guys hunting you, I knew you'd head straight for the hideout. So, here I am!"

Justin was amazed. "But...how did you know? About Grady and the invisibility shield? I never said anything!"

"I'm your twin, Justin!" Jenny whispered scornfully. "I knew the minute you started acting so weird that you were mixed up in another of your mysteries. Besides, I recognized that sandy-haired man you were talking to at soccer practice. He was the same guy you said had been following us that day on the wharf."

She added slyly, "The same day you disappeared and came back talking about 'national security'! So I figured the guy must be a government agent. When Dad got so mad about that invisibility thing, I guessed someone must be trying to steal it. I didn't know what you were up to, but I figured you must be helping that sandy-haired guy."

"But how in the world did you know Grady was a traitor?" Justin demanded. He added bitterly, "He sure fooled me!"

"I didn't really," Jenny admitted. "Not till I heard you talking with those guys. But I knew something was wrong when you were determined Abdul was a spy. Dad had told me once about Abdul—how he's worked so hard to bring health care and modern technology and all that to his country. *And* how he got shot once by Muslim terrorists who didn't like what he was doing!"

Jenny shifted her legs to a more comfortable position. "Anyway, that didn't sound like a spy to me." She added, "I still don't know why everyone's after Dad's project. When we get out of here, you're going to tell me everything that's happened!"

"If we do get out." Justin said sourly. He was impressed at the way Jenny had pieced everything together, but he felt foolish. He'd been so sure he'd sidetracked his twin.

"Look, Jenny, we're in big trouble! No one knows where we are, and Grady's bound to find us come morning. I wish you'd thought to call Mom and Dad or something!"

"Oh, did I leave that out?" Jenny said innocently. Justin could feel her smiling in the dark. "I *did* call—after I untied that park ranger! Dad said they'd be here as soon as Mr. Ramirez—that's the NSA agent that was arresting Dad—could scrape up a helicopter. He said to sit tight until they show up."

Justin was speechless. Finding his voice at last, he said in a fervent whisper, "Jenny, did I ever tell you you're the greatest!"

"Not often enou—" Jenny grabbed her brother's arm. But he'd already heard the voices. Grady and his men were sweeping back through this part of the woods!

"There's no sign of him." Hacker complained just beyond the brush that cloaked the hideout. "Can't this wait till morning?"

"You'll keep searching till he's found!" Grady's voice was unsympathetic. "That is, if you want your share of ten million."

The murmur of voices faded. Then, from somewhere across the clearing, Justin heard Grady call, "I'm going to check that ranger. You three split up and search the south end of the island! If you find him, let off a shot!"

Jenny whispered, "If Grady finds the ranger loose, he'll know we've called for help!"

Justin nodded. "We've got to warn the ranger!"

Jenny slithered head first through the narrow opening of the den. Justin waited for the soft whistle that was their all-clear signal before he followed, reluctantly leaving the wool blanket behind. He shivered as the chill of the winter night bit into his damp clothing.

The bobbing gleam of the searchers' flashlights faded into the distance. Grabbing hands, the two picked their way across the clearing. When they reached the woods, Jenny took the lead, slipping with ghost-like silence from tree to tree.

It didn't take long to reach the hiking trail that led down to the docks. With Grady already ahead of them and the other three men searching the far side of the island, the chance of being seen was small. They'd have to take that chance if they were to reach the park ranger in time! They began to run.

The pair had just reached the back yard of the ranger's house when Justin caught the sound of angry voices inside. As they crept along the side of the house, there was a muffled thud, then a groan.

"The park ranger said he had a shotgun!" Jenny whispered hopefully. "Maybe he caught Grady!"

Justin shook his head. He didn't think the renegade NSA agent was the sort to be taken unaware by a park ranger! Reaching the window where he had earlier spied on Grady and his men, he peeked in cautiously.

It was just as he'd feared! Grady stood across the living room, the young park ranger sprawled at his feet. With a groan, the ranger rolled over. Pushing himself to his hands and knees, he dove at Grady's legs. But Grady stepped to one side, kicking the ranger in the face. The ranger crashed to the floor.

The renegade agent kicked the groaning park ranger in the ribs. Then, pulling a gun from under his jacket, he leveled the weapon at the ranger's head.

"Who were you calling?" he demanded harshly. "And who cut you free?"

"We've got to help him!" Jenny whispered, her eyes wide with horror.

But Justin had stiffened with sudden excitement. Tapping Jenny on the shoulder, he pointed. Not far from the window, hidden from Grady's view, lay a double-barreled shotgun. A phone dangled by its receiver over the side of a table.

Justin studied the layout of the room. If only they could get that gun! A dark doorway on the far side of the room gave him an idea. "There's got to be a back door!" he whispered to Jenny. "I'll get Grady to come after me! Then you can go in the back and grab that gun!"

"You get the gun." Jenny whispered back. "You're the one who knows how to use it. I'll distract Grady."

Justin knew Jenny disliked guns and had refused to learn to shoot. But he protested, "No, it's too dangerous! What if he catches you?"

Jenny started toward the front door, pausing only to hiss, "Hurry up! There's no time to argue!"

Justin didn't waste any more time. He raced around the back of the house. The back door was unlocked! Easing it open, he stepped inside. The light was off, but the faint gleam of a refrigerator and stove told him he was in the kitchen.

Crossing the kitchen, he peered into the living room. Grady still stood in front of the fireplace. The park ranger lay motionless at his feet. *Were they too late after all?*

Then he heard a loud knock at the front door. Jenny's diversion!

"Who's there?" Grady stepped away from the park ranger, his gun held steady in one hand, barrel pointed toward the ceiling. When no one answered, he started with purposeful strides for the front door.

Good job, Jenny! Now run for it! Dropping to his hands and knees, Justin crawled rapidly across the room. But he had several feet left to go when another impatient pounding rang out. Grady yanked open the door and Justin bit back a cry of dismay as his sister stumbled into the room, her hand still raised for another knock.

Grabbing Jenny by the shoulder, Grady pulled her farther into the room. Slipping his gun into a shoulder holster, he pushed her dark curls away from her face. "You're the Parker girl! Justin's sis—"

The renegade agent whirled around and reached for his gun. But Justin dove for the shotgun. Snatching it up, he leveled it over the back of the armchair.

"Drop the gun, Grady!" he ordered sharply. "Let her go, or I'll shoot!"

Grady pushed Jenny away from him, but he didn't drop the gun. To Justin's horror, the renegade agent began walking slowly toward him, his gun hanging loose in his hand.

"I don't think so, Justin." Grady spoke pleasantly, but his eyes were narrowed and hard. "You're not the type to shoot a man in cold blood."

"But I am!" a grim voice broke in from behind him. "Drop the gun!"

Grady spun around, his features twisted with anger. The park ranger was on his feet. Blood masked one eye, but the small pistol in the other hand was trained rock-steady on Grady. The bottom drawer of a nearby desk stood open.

With a snarl, Grady let his gun slip through his fingers to the floor. Darting forward, Jenny grabbed the weapon and pointed it gingerly at Grady. The park ranger wiped blood from his eyes. With his gun, he motioned toward an armchair. "You! Sit!"

Grady scanned the three guns leveled at him. Then he shrugged and obeyed. The park ranger turned to Justin. "Think you can tie up our friend here? You'll find the rope they used on me in the corner."

"Sure!" Justin answered.

He started across the room, the shotgun turned barrel-up in one hand. Without thinking, he passed between the park ranger and their prisoner. In that brief instant, Grady sprang and Justin was pinned to the ground. Grady's heavy body knocked the wind out of Justin and those steel-strong hands tried to tear the shotgun from his grip.

Bang! An explosion rocked the room. In the same instant, Grady lurched up in surprise and Justin slipped from his grasp and scrambled to his feet. The shotgun was still in his hands and hadn't been fired. Justin gasped for breath and looked across the room. The park ranger had his gun pointed straight at Grady, but he nodded his head toward Jenny. Jenny's face was white as she stared down at the smoking gun in her hand. Her stunned eyes then looked up to the ceiling. There was a hole directly above her.

"Let's try this again, son," said the ranger. "This time you give me the gun first." Then he nodded to Grady, "And *you* get back in that chair!"

Justin gladly handed over the shotgun, careful not to get between the ranger and Grady this time. He then tied Grady securely to the armchair, using so many knots they would need to cut the rope to get him loose. Justin tied the last knot and stepped back. That's when he noticed a gleam of satisfaction in Grady's cold, steel-grey eyes.

Something's wrong, thought Justin.

"That gunshot!" exclaimed Jenny. "Remember—Grady said to fire a shot if they found you!"

Justin caught the flash of anger on Grady's face. "Now they'll think Grady's got me! They might be on their way right now!"

The park ranger wiped his hand across his blood-streaked face. "At least two of them have guns! We're in trouble!"

Justin looked around the room, then down at their prisoner. "Maybe not!" he said slowly. "I have an idea!"

Five minutes later, Justin cast a satisfied glance around the room. Jenny had already slipped into the kitchen. Grady sat facing the fire, his armchair turned at an angle so the ropes wouldn't be visible from the door. Several layers of clear tape provided an invisible gag. The park ranger lay in a huddle at his feet.

Justin had just stepped behind the drapes when he heard running steps outside. A moment later, the door slammed open. Hacker and the two terrorists crowded into the room.

Hacker stopped short when he saw Grady's silhouette. "So you're taking a rest while we're out freezing!" he exclaimed angrily. "Where's the kid?"

"Right here!" Justin stepped out from behind the curtains, swinging the shotgun to cover the three men. The park ranger jumped to his feet and ordered, "Get your hands up, or I'll shoot!"

"Don't even think about it!" Jenny moved in from the kitchen. She held Grady's gun steady with both hands, pretending she knew what she was doing. One of the men hastily dropped his hand away from his jacket. Justin tried not to grin as the two Muslim terrorists tossed their weapons to the carpet. *If they only knew that the safety was on his gun!*

"Now you three slowly back up against that wall and don't move a muscle!" commanded the ranger. He and Justin kept their weapons pointed at them as Jenny carefully picked up their discarded guns with shaking hands.

"Now all we have to do is wait for that boat to show up," she said, trying to sound brave as she laid the guns at the ranger's feet. "Won't Dad be surprised!"

Justin just finished the last knot on his three new prisoners when an amused voice said, "Anyone here need help?"

"Dad!" Forgetting the men she was helping to guard, Jenny hurled herself across the room. Justin dropped the end of the rope and sighed in relief.

Dad glanced around the room, one eyebrow raised. "Well, it looks like you two have everything under control!"

Only then did Justin notice the two men who had entered the living room behind his father. Mr. Ramirez, the NSA agent who had driven the brown van, crossed the room to look down at Grady, still gagged.

"If it isn't O'Brian!" Mr. Ramirez said. He shook his head as his gaze moved from the renegade agent to the other three prisoners. "Who in the world will ever believe Grady O'Brian was brought down by a couple of kids!"

Grady's eyes burned with hatred. Still grinning, Mr. Ramirez strolled over to the three Parkers. Turning to Justin, he said, "I've only got one question right now. *Where are the plans for the GP145?*"

In the last hour Justin had completely forgotten about the black pouch. Unzipping his wet jacket, he reached inside. "They're safe!" he said proudly. "On these disks—"

Justin pulled out the pouch and felt a sloshing inside the bag. Turning it over, he stared with horror at the small slit in the zip-lock closure that kept it watertight. Somewhere in all the crashing and scraping in the sea and on the rocks, the black pouch must have torn open!

Grabbing the pouch from Justin's hands, Mr. Ramirez turned it upside down. A stream of water spilled to the floor. The NSA agent pulled out a red disk.

"This disk is ruined!" he said tightly, holding up the dripping, square of plastic. "We've lost the GP145 plans for good!"

chapter sixteen

Dad took the ruined disk from Mr. Ramirez and turned it over in his hands. "This is worthless, all right!" Dad glanced over at Justin and sighed.

Justin looked down at the floor. *If only I hadn't been so stupid!* he thought. Dad placed a hand on his son's shoulder and smiled sadly.

"Don't blame yourself, Justin. It wasn't your fault. And besides, thanks to you, we're rounding up a whole network of spies and international terrorists!"

"But, Dad, I—"

"Not now, Justin—" Dad held up his hand as the roar of a motorboat drowned out Justin's attempted explanation. This was followed by heavy boots thudding up the boardwalk from the docks.

The arrivals turned out to be the police reinforcements Mr. Ramirez had requested earlier. Justin didn't have another chance to speak with his father until the four prisoners were escorted to the police boat under the supervision of the other NSA agent. The park ranger, despite strong protests, was also dispatched to the hospital, and Mr. Ramirez assigned a police sergeant to keep watch on the island until the park service could be notified.

When the three Parkers were alone with Mr. Ramirez, Justin turned once again to Dad. "I'm really sorry about those disks, Dad, but—"

Dad interrupted again, this time with a big hug. "Justin, I

know how badly you feel about this. You don't have to keep apologizing—"

"I'm afraid it's not as easy as that!" Mr. Ramirez broke in sternly. "Justin has been involved in a federal crime. We're going to need some explanations."

Justin swallowed hard. *What kind of trouble was he in?* But Mr. Ramirez didn't appear too angry as he motioned them to sit on the sofa. He pulled an armchair closer and began, "Start at the beginning, Justin. Tell me exactly how you first got involved with Grady O'Brian."

It took Justin a long time to tell his story. Mr. Ramirez scribbled notes in a small black notebook, interrupting often to demand more specific details. Dad tightened his arm around Justin's shoulders when he explained how Grady had threatened Dad's arrest to get Justin to work for him.

"Then, tonight when Mr. Ramirez said they'd traced the copies to your computer…well, I knew I'd really gotten you into trouble! I figured they'd arrest you if I couldn't get Grady to say it was his idea."

"Justin, I was in no danger of being arrested." Dad broke in gently. "When the investigators checked with my secretary and the guard at the front gate, they found that I hadn't even been in the office at the time the computer logged those copies. But after they induced Miss Pettigrew to talk, they found out that *you* had been in my office. And since Mr. Ramirez had seen you with Grady, who was already under investigation…well they just put two and two together…"

Justin felt like such a fool. *How could he have fallen for such lies?*

Dad shook his head, "What I just don't get is…how in the world did you ever figure out my password?"

Justin explained how he'd worked out the password and made the copies. "I'm sorry I lied to you, Dad. I…I thought I had to, but I know now that I was wrong!"

"You're forgiven, Justin." Dad's eyes were suspiciously bright.

"You thought you were helping me—and your country." He cleared his throat. "But next time, son, give me credit for being a little harder to fool. And always remember—if an adult asks you to keep a secret from your parents—you can bet something's wrong. You come tell me right away!"

Justin nodded sheepishly and completed his story. Then Jenny explained her part in the evening's events. Just as she finished, Justin looked over at Mr. Ramirez. He felt stupid for assuming that Mr. Ramirez was an Arab terrorist just because of his olive complexion. *How ridiculous to judge a person by his skin color!*

"I'm sorry I ran away from you," he told Mr. Ramirez. "I thought you were trying to steal the plans." Justin rubbed his eyes with his hands. "I was such an idiot! I believed everything Grady told me!"

"Don't feel too badly!" Mr. Ramirez answered with unexpected kindness. "Grady O'Brian has fooled a lot of older and more experienced heads than yours! The truth is, Grady *was* an NSA agent at one time. He was one of the best! I worked with him a couple of times when I first joined the agency, and I can tell you he could talk the head of the Russian KGB into turning over state secrets! But he decided there was more money on the other side of the law."

Mr. Ramirez slammed his notebook shut and continued. "Grady used old military contacts from his Agency days to find out about the GP145. That's how he found out about a young computer genius who had been fired from the project for using his computer skills to steal classified information."

"Hacker!" exclaimed Justin.

Dad snapped his fingers. "That's where I've seen his face before! He wasn't in my department, or I'd have recognized him right off."

"Hacker wanted revenge *and* money!" Mr. Ramirez explained. "It was easy enough for Grady to talk him into pooling resources. The Arab Front for World Liberation had already offered Grady ten million dollars for the GP145. The plan was for Hacker to use his knowledge of the Boeing security system to break into the mainframe computer and steal the invisibility shield. But there had been too many changes in the system since Hacker left. Grady and Hacker needed help inside Boeing to get those plans. Justin was a piece of luck they hadn't expected."

Justin flushed red as the NSA agent turned his sharp gaze on him. Dad seemed to sense Justin's embarrassment and added, "Well, at least you saved the plans from falling into enemy hands, Justin! If you hadn't been there, Grady would have found another way to break into Boeing. And we might not have been able to stop him!" But Dad sighed as he added heavily, "I'll have to call my superiors and let them know that the GP145 is completely gone. The invisibility shield project is a total loss!"

"But, Dad!" began Justin, this time without interruption. "That's what I've been trying to tell you! The plans *aren't* gone!"

"Maybe with enough time, we can duplicate—" Dad swiveled around to stare at his son. "What did you say, Justin?"

"I said, the plans *aren't* gone! Grady had me make *two* copies of the GP145. He told me to bring all the disks in that black pouch, but..." Justin looked at his father, "when I found out that all your files were destroyed, well...I didn't know if Grady was responsible. But I just couldn't give him the only copies left of the project. I mean, what if something happened to him? Besides, those were *your* plans. Anyway, I figured he only needed one copy!"

Dad gripped Justin's shoulder tightly. "Are you telling me you have the other copy of those plans?"

Justin nodded. "I was afraid Mr. Ramirez here would find it if I left it in the house. Remember, I thought he was one of the bad guys so..." Justin paused dramatically and caught his breath.

Jenny nudged him impatiently. "Com'on, Justin! Where is it?"

He shrugged nonchalantly, but his grin almost split his freckled cheeks. "I stuck it in the mail. Dad should get it tomorrow afternoon—that is, unless you want to break into the mailbox down near the ferry terminal. It should still be there. The next pick-up is tomorrow morning."

The stunned reaction from Justin's audience was almost worth all the pain that had brought him to this point. The two men sat speechlessly staring, and then Jenny let out a war whoop. "Way to go, Justin!"

Mr. Ramirez leaned over and shook his hand. "Justin, that was brilliant! I take back all the things I thought about you these past few days when I was chasing you and Grady around the city." He rose to his feet and said, "Excuse me, while I make a phone call. I think I have enough influence to get that mailbox opened tonight."

Mr. Ramirez flipped open his cellular phone and gave a few clipped orders. Then he turned back to the three Parkers. His sharp gaze softened as he seemed to take in for the first time Justin's still wet and torn clothing. His socks were shredded and what showed of his feet looked bruised and swollen.

"It's time we get you three home," said Mr. Ramirez. "Justin's been through more than enough for one night!"

This time Justin enjoyed the boat ride across the Sound. He had borrowed one of the heavy winter coats from the ranger's house. Curled warm and snug next to Jenny in the cabin of the small boat, he watched sleepily as the pointed prow cut sound-lessly through the waves toward the glittering lights of Seattle. The unusual quiet was due to the electric engine that had allowed the NSA agents to reach the island unheard. Justin was just dropping off to sleep when the electronic buzz of Mr. Ramirez' cellular phone startled him awake.

"They located the disk!" exclaimed Mr. Ramirez. "They're already booting the material back into the Boeing computer. And it all seems to be there!"

"Thank God!" Dad let out a war whoop just like Jenny's and grabbed Justin. "Son, I don't know how to thank you. You've done your country and Boeing an enormous service. Not to mention saving my job!"

"Would you have really lost your job, if they hadn't gotten the plans back?" asked Jenny. "Even if it wasn't you who stole them?"

"Probably. Since it was my own son, and my password that Grady used to break into the mainframe computer."

Justin was glad he hadn't known the risk to his father's job any sooner. But this wasn't the last revelation for the evening. When the three Parkers arrived back home they were met by Mom at the front door. After some brief hugging and sincere scolding, Mom pulled Dad aside.

"Ron, you have a visitor," she whispered urgently. "He says you are expecting him."

"Abdul!" Dad slapped his forehead. "He's flying out tonight. I promised him a ride to the airport!"

With long strides, he led the way inside. Abdul el Kutub was waiting for them in the living room. Looking exotic as ever in his flowing white robes and jeweled turban, he swept across the room to give Dad a smacking kiss on each cheek.

"Your wife told me there was trouble—great danger!" Abdul exclaimed throwing his hands up with horror. "I am so glad to see that you and your children are safe!"

The Arab visitor turned to bow to Jenny, and Justin tugged on Dad's arm, "Dad, I've got to talk to you," he whispered. "It's about Abdul!"

Dad glanced over at Abdul who was paying Jenny an extravagant compliment, then back to Justin. "What is it, son?"

"It's just...there's something I still don't understand," Justin spoke in a low voice. "I know they said Abdul wasn't really a spy. But, well...I heard your phone call. I really was going to tell you about Grady then, but when you said that you really were passing information to Abdul—"

Dad looked completely puzzled. "Justin, you're going to have to start over. What phone call?"

"You said you'd gotten the data from the Boeing computer." Justin quickly repeated everything he could recall from that eavesdropped conversation. "You said you were going to work in his country—that you'd been keeping it a secret. You were afraid we'd be upset…I thought…" he finished lamely. "I don't know what I thought."

Dad threw back his head and laughed, but Justin couldn't see what was so funny. Dad continued to laugh and Justin folded his arms across his chest and frowned. Finally Dad wiped his eyes.

"I know you don't know what's so funny, Justin," began Dad, still smiling. Everyone in the room was listening now. "And I can understand how you could have misinterpreted my words." He turned to Abdul. "The disks I passed on to my friend, Abdul, were completely authorized by Boeing. They just contained some unclassified technical information—engine specifications and airplane maintenance manuals. It's all part of our program to offer technical support to less-developed countries." Dad slapped Abdul on the back, "I met Abdul through this program. His father is a sheik who controls a large area of his country. The first time I met Abdul, I shared my faith in Jesus Christ with him. I helped him find an Arabic Bible and he began to read and study it. Now, whenever he visits Seattle, he comes to me with more questions about the Christian faith."

Justin nodded. For the most part it made sense. "But what about what you said about working in his country—and keeping it a secret?"

Dad chuckled. "Well, I guess it's time to let you and Jenny in on something your mother and I have been discussing." He motioned them all over to the chairs. "You see, we have always been interested in missions. You know how often we have missionaries over, and how we support missions in other countries. But we've always dreamed of doing more!"

Justin and Jenny both listened with wide-eyed interest. Dad continued explaining, "I'm no great preacher, but I've wondered if there was some way I could use my computer skills to serve God. Some months back, I had a chance to visit with a representative of a mission called Christian Technicians International— or CTI. It's a group of Christian electronic technicians who help missionaries and Christian relief organizations around the world to set up computer equipment and programs to assist in their ministries."

Dad glanced across at Abdul's big smile. "Then I met Abdul! In his country, missionaries aren't allowed to preach the Gospel. But Abdul has talked his father into allowing Christian doctors and nurses to come in to set up clinics and teach health care to his people. CTI technicians would set up the computers and equipment necessary. But Abdul wanted me to be the one to come to his country."

Dad looked at Mom. "At first, I told Abdul that I couldn't go—not with my job and family responsibilities. But I started praying about it, and God began to open the doors. Boeing agreed to give me a six-month leave from my job. CTI accepted me to work with them—not just in Abdul's country, but any-where they need help. I know how hard it has been for you to get used to your new school this year. I didn't want to worry you with another change until there was a real possibility that we would go."

A twinkle crept into Dad's eyes as he looked from Justin to Jenny. "Well, kids? How do you feel about a few months on the other side of the Atlantic? It would mean studying by correspon-dence—since there wouldn't be any English-speaking schools. And I can't even say where we'll be from one week to the next—Saudi Arabia, Egypt, Israel, Russia—wherever we're needed. Would you be willing to go?"

Go! Exchanging excited glances, Justin and Jenny both burst out, "Of course we want to go!"

Jenny turned eagerly to Abdul. "Does this mean we'll be stay-ing in your house? Will we meet your son and daughter—the ones that are our ages?" Justin leaned back and listened as the babble of excited conversation broke out around him. Even as tired as he was after this most recent adventure he could still get excited about what might be ahead. *A camel caravan across the desert? The mysterious pyramids and temples of Egypt? Maybe he might even walk in Jesus' footsteps in the Old City of Jerusalem!*

Justin's eyelids drooped as one exotic scene chased another through his mind. Africa, the Middle East—who cares where they went first? There was a whole exciting world just waiting out there!